This book is due for return on or before the last date shown below.

1

JUSTINE
MARQUIS DE SADE
TRANSLATION PIERALESSANDRAO CASAVINI

FIRST PUBLISHED 1791
TRANSLATION FIRST PUBLISHED 1953 BY
THE OLYMPIA PRESS
REPRINTED 1963 AS #67 OF THE
TRAVELLER'S COMPANION SERIES

2005 OLYMPIA PRESS.COM
ISBN: 1-59654-176-8

THE OLYMPIA PRESS.
A DVISION OF DISRUPTIVE PUBLISHING, INC.

Chapter 1

THERE WERE two sisters very unlike each other. The elder, Juliet, was not yet sixteen, but already was as worldly-wise and sly as a woman of thirty. Moreover, she was inordinately vain, and frivolous and bold. Her firm supple figure and fine dark eyes lent her an attractiveness which was too soon brought to her own attention, and she had all the makings of a consummate coquette. On the other hand, Justine, her younger sister, was a modest, timid and ingenuous young creature; and just as Juliet was gay, wanton and unprincipled, so Justine was serious, melancholy and profuse with fine upright sentiments. But Justine was far less precocious; and her artless simplicity led her into many snares and pitfalls.

They came from a good old family of wealth and influence. Their father was a prominent banker in Paris. Brought up in one of the most celebrated abbeys in the country, they both had the very best of tutors, companions and books, and such an abundance of comforts that little else could have been desired.

But before long everything to these two young girls was irretrievably lost. Their father was thrown into penury by a sudden and serious bankruptcy, and overcome with despair he committed suicide; his wife died soon after.

Time was when both sisters had lavished upon them by a host of friends and relatives every kindness and consideration, but now with the family fortune and their inheritance changed so radically for the worse they were despised and ignored on all sides. Young as they were, none of their uncles or aunts wished to be bothered with two such beggarly orphans—nor anybody else for that matter—and they were thrown out into the world, almost penniless, to shift for themselves.

Juliet, carefree and gay, desired nothing better than her

freedom. Though young and inexperienced and friendless, alone in the world, she was quite indifferent to the disastrous reverses which had just occurred; and was delighted with the sudden prospect of being her own mistress. She was really glad to be rid at last of all restraint, looking forward with avid eagerness to a life of complete freedom and indulgence unhampered by any parental yoke. And at last she could also joyfully anticipate opportunities for realizing more satisfyingly, and to the full, strange physical feelings that came to her as yet but vaguely—feelings she always thought so nice, and that had stirred her restless over-ripe curiosity and too often disturbed deeply her premature imagination. But Justine, overwhelmed by the tragedy of their position, sank into a heavy cloud of gloom, and had grown so lackadaisical that Juliet freely prodded her with the butt of her sarcasms for becoming too easily a prey to tender emotions. Justine wilted with horror before the brazen callousness of her sister's words, who said that there was little use worrying over anything not really after all affecting them personally, as it was possible to find within themselves physical pleasures keen enough to wipe out all suffering and unhappiness, and that it was more urgent to redouble one's pleasure than increase one's pain; in short, that they ought to do anything to deaden such emotions as brought them nothing but sorrow. With their youth and fine figures, it was impossible, anyway, for them to starve. Could they not get somebody to keep them, and live in luxury and comfort? And she also poured ridicule on Justine's belief that it was only holy wedlock that made a young girl happy. On the contrary, as a captive under the laws of matrimony, would she not suffer much and be miserable? But if they were to abandon themselves to prostitution they could, at least, assure themselves of money, variety and love's delights!

Justine was scandalized by this sort of talk and said she

4

preferred death to such disgrace; and the moment she saw her sister decided upon a life that made her shudder she made up her mind to live with her no longer.

Their intentions so opposed, they separated as amicably as possible without definitely promising to see each other again. How could Juliet, who wished to become a grand dame, any longer associate with a little girl whose virtuous and simple inclinations might embarrass her? And could Justine risk her honor in the society of a perverse creature who was about to take up a career of public debauchery? And so they parted and each went her own separate way.

Chapter 2

NOW THAT HER SISTER, Juliet, was gone out of her life, Justine felt more than ever alone and forsaken. And so forlorn did she become, and her difficulties so extreme, that in spite of her skittishness she soon realized the immediate need of having to appeal to somebody for help. Though at first she could think of no one to turn to, the name of a woman who at one time had been her mother's dressmaker and always shown great friendliness in the past later came into her mind, and to her Justine decided to go and for the sake of old times ask assistance. She was sure her old friend would help her. But she learned soon enough how little in the mood this woman was to listen to the troubles of others; and was crestfallen and discouraged on being turned away with little ceremony from the rude woman's door.

"Oh heavens!" cried the poor little creature, "must my first steps in this world be so disheartening! This woman loved me once, why does she despise me now? Are people respected only by the gains others can get from them?"

As her last resort, she then went to a noted politician. She was dressed in a little white frock, her lovely hair carelessly bound up under a large bonnet, and her throat, barely showing, was hidden under two or three ells of gauze. Her face because of the sorrows which were eating her up was wan; and two tears stood in her eyes, giving them a still sadder and more tender expression. When she arrived before the friend she described her misfortunes to him in tears.

"You behold me, sir.... you behold me in a very sad state!" she said. "I have lost my father and mother. Heaven took them from me at an age when I needed them most. They died poor, sir, and I have nothing... here is all they left," showing her palms with a little money in it, "and not a place to rest my poor head! Take pity on me! take pity! You are a friend of the people, those who are always the pearl of my heart! In the name of God whom I adore, tell me what to do, what's to become of me!"

Having carefully feasted his greedy eyes all along the graceful budding outlines of her fragile little person, the great man replied that the country was burdened enough and it was impossible to give further alms; but if Justine would do the rough work, there would always be a piece of bread for her in the kitchen; and while saying this he slightly lifted up her chin and gave her a kiss she thought far too worldly for a diplomat. Instinctively she repulsed him and said, "I ask nothing from you, neither charity nor a servant's place! I only want advice, which my youth and misfortunes need. But you wish to make me purchase them a little too dear!"

At this, he drove her quickly away, abashed and alarmed at being uncovered as more rascal than statesman.

Near the end of her resources, the unhappy girl then entered a rooming house, rented a small miserably furnished attic, and there abandoned herself to her woes and tears.

The small patrimony left to her when her father died Justine soon completely exhausted, and her distress grew more and more acute. And the more was her need, the less help and kindness, it seemed, did she receive.

Of all the trials and rebuffs she suffered at this early period of her life, of all the proposals made her, the one she experienced at the hands of Mr. Dubourg, one of the richest men of the city, was most characteristic. He was recommended to Justine by the woman at whose house she was stopping as a man whose generosity and kindness would most surely help her.

Justine lost no time in going to see him. When she arrived at his house she had to wait very long in his antechamber before getting an audience with him. But she was finally admitted to his room, just as he had gotten out of bed, wrapped in a loose morning gown which barely hid his body, and was ready to be attended to by his valet; whom he dismissed, and asked what she wanted. "Alas!" she answered, confused, "I am a poor orphan, hardly fifteen, and already I know the bitterness of misfortune. I beg you have pity on me... please.... I beg you!"

She then gave him a lengthy account of all her troubles, the difficulties finding work, also, not being born for it, the shame she felt taking any menial job. And she told him the hope she had that he would help her in some way, that he would find work for her. After listening to her with many interruptions, Mr. Dubourg then asked her were she a good girl.

"I would not be so hard-pressed, sir, were I otherwise!"

"By what right, then, do you expect the rich to help you if you will not serve them?"

"What way do you expect me to serve them? I wish nothing better than to do what is proper."

"The help of a child like you is little use in a house. You're not old enough or strong enough to be employed as you wish. You'd better busy yourself pleasing men. Try and find someone who will keep you. This virtue you value so is worthless in this world; you may guard it ever so much, it will not feed you. What men respect least, what they despise most, is virtue in your sex. They value, here, my child, only what brings profit and enjoyment. What profits us woman's virtue! Their willingness serves and delights us, but their chastity doesn't interest us in the least. When men like myself give, it is always with the hope of receiving something in return. How can a little girl like you repay me for what I can do for you?"

"Oh, sir, is there no charity or kindness among men!"

"Very little! It is only much talked about. Why should it be otherwise? People, sensibly, no longer oblige other gratis; they have discovered that the pleasures of charity were but the enjoyment of pride. And since pride is a mere illusion, they now seek for more tangible sensations. For instance, they have learned that with a girl like you it is far better to reap all the pleasures love can bring than those very unsatisfying ones of helping her for nothing. The pleasures of sympathy and generosity are not worth even the slightest pleasure of the senses."

"Sir!" said Justine, "with principles like these the unfortunate must perish!"

"What difference would that make! There are more people than are wanted in the country, anyway. What difference does it make if there are more or fewer individuals?"

"Do you believe children could respect their parents if they were thus treated by them?" Justine asked.

"What do children mean to a father when they trouble him!"

"They'd be better off smothered in the cradle!" she retorted.

"Of course! Such was the very custom in many countries. Such was the custom among the Greeks; and such it is among the Chinese, where weak, helpless children are constantly put to death. Why let such creatures live? orphans, bastards arid cripples only burden the State with a commodity of which it has too much already. But let us drop this

8

talk, my child, which you can't seem to understand. Why complain of your lot when it depends upon yourself to remedy it?"

"At what price, good heavens?" Justine sighed. "At the price of that virtue which has no other value than the one your pride sets upon it. That's all I can do for you. Agree to it or get out!" He rose and flung open the door. "I hate beggars!" he added.

Justine fell to whimpering, but instead of softening him her tears irritated him; and he shut the door again and seizing her brutally by the collar of her dress said he was going to force her to do what she refused him willingly. But at this desperate moment her grave danger fired her courage and she tore herself from his hands and made a wild rush for the door. "Beast!" she yelled, "may Heaven punish you as you deserve... you are not worthy of the air you breathe!"

She ran almost all the way home to tell her landlady the brutal way she was received. But to Justine's surprise she was greeted with a shower of insults for her discourtesy to Mr. Dubourg.

"You stupid little ass!" this woman said to her, "do you imagine that men are dupes to give charity to girls like you without getting their money's worth! Mr. Dubourg was very kind to have acted the way he did. In his place I should not have let you go without at least satisfying myself. But since you will not take advantage of the help I find for you, do as you please; but pay me the money you owe me at once or go to jail!"

"Oh, please take pity on me!" Justine implored.

"Sure enough, pity!... one can starve on pity!"

"What do you expect me to do?"

"You must go back to him. You must please him. You must bring me back some money! I'll see him and try to fix matters up. But mind you, you must behave like a lady!"

Desperate and without any other alternative, Justine

became resigned to the fate hanging over her and suffered her landlady to go and see the great financier. When her landlady returned she told Justine that she found the great gentleman terribly enraged; and that only after much pleading and coaxing she prevailed upon him to relent and agree to see her next morning. "She didn't treat me right—she made me so unhappy!" Mr. Dubourg complained. And Justine was given careful directions so as to be sure to conduct herself properly and obey him in every respect.

The next morning, in a great fear, she arrived again at the home of Mr. Dubourg whom she found alone, and was welcomed with much sullenness.

"You can thank your landlady," he said to her very harshly, "for the kindness I show you today. After yesterday you ought to realize how unworthy you are of any kindness at all. Now take your things off, and if you show the slightest resistance to me today god knows what I'll do to you!"

She threw herself at his knees and cried, "Oh, have pity! Be generous enough to help me without taking from me what I value more than my life. Yes, I'd rather die a thousand times than sacrifice my virtue.... Sir! sir! do not force me, please, please!... oh! oh! will you find happiness amid tears and disgust!... can you expect pleasure where you shall only find hatred!... as soon as you shall finish your crime, the sight of my sorrow will surely fill you with remorse!..."

But to have propitiated a man who found in her grief only a greater stimulant to his passion was more than even Justine could have hoped for; and the financier, inflamed by the bitterness of her cries, decided to bring matters promptly to a head. Getting up in a state in which all his reason was lost, and any resistance but a goad to his delirium, he savagely lay hold of her, and tore away her hands, which were hindering him; and by turns he abused, flattered, caressed, pinched and bit her. It was a strange medley of lusts: and if Mr. Dubourg had been less eager he would surely have dishonored Virtue. But she owed her deliverance to the man's extravagances; for in spite of the delay and his difficulty caused by the complexity of his enterprises, the effervescence of his desire was unexpectedly hurried, and the strength of his passion suddenly extinguished. His surprise was so great, and his disappointment so keen, that he blamed Justine for his own weakness, and become more abusive and insolent with her.

Everything having miscarried, he wished to rekindle himself by fresh overtures and abuses, more mortifying and painful to her: there was nothing he did not try, nothing he did not say to her. Her awkwardness especially angered him. However, her submission failed to excite him, and somehow he tired again without being able to regain what was necessary for his designs and finally gave up. But he made her promise to come next day, and to secure this promise he gave her only a very small sum of money.

Justine returned home, humbled by the adventure and firmly resolved never to see him again. And she cursed the brute who so cruelly took advantage of her misery.

Chapter 3

MANY MONTHS passed. Justine, half-starved, in no less bitter a plight, gradually sunk into a listless apathy and let things take their course. She was still staying at the same dreary rooming house. Though her landlady kept pestering her for money and harassing her with threats and abuse, she never actually put her out into the street. The old frowzy woman made good use of Justine instead; and put her to all sorts of drab labor, making her sweep and clean to pay off the rent and a small daily allowance of black bread and occasionally some thin soup.

Often during those long, wretched weeks Justine sought to recover traces of Juliet, to whom she now looked as her only hope of salvation from her present misery; and many the night she strolled through the street staring closely into the faces of passers-by, hoping to espy the familiar face of her sister again. But the search was fruitless, and she eventually gave up in despair.

One day the landlady came to her and said that at last she found work for her.

"Oh, heavens!" Justine cried, throwing herself with happiness into her arms.

The man she was to serve was a Parisian usurer called Mr. Hairpin, who got rich not only by lending money at high interest but also by cheating poor helpless people whenever he could. He lived in the poorest quarter of the city with an old crone of fifty whom he sometimes called his wife.

When Justine entered his household he took her aside and gave her a long interview. He insisted on calling her Therese, which he said he preferred to the name of Justine.

"Therese," he said to her, "the primary virtue of my house is honesty. If you ever so much as steal a penny I will have you hanged—you understand, my child? You see, the little pleasures we enjoy, my wife and I, are the fruit of our long toil and constant sobriety. Do you eat much, my darling?"

"A few slices of bread a day, sir," Justine said, "and some water and a little soup, whenever I can get any."

"Soup? soup?... what's this I hear?—Look here!" Mr. Hairpin said, turning to his wife, "gaze upon the progress of luxury! That thing has starved for a year, and that thing wants soup! Why, even on Sundays we seldom have any; and we work like galley slaves. My dear, we'll give you three slices of bread a day, and every now and then a bottle of clean river-water. And if you are economical and we are satisfied with your services, at the end of the year my wife will give you her old gown and I'll give you a few francs to the bargain. Oh, you'll find almost nothing to do here— why, it can be done at a glance. All you have to do is wash, sweep and clean these six rooms only three times a week;

and also, make our bed; answer the door; powder my wig; coif my wife; take care of my dog and parrot; look after the kitchen; polish the cutlery; help my wife prepare the food; and then spend four or five hours a day in making linen, stockings, caps and other such little household trifles; and that's about all. You see, Therese, you'll have lots of time for yourself; which will let you do as you please, provided of course, my child, that you are good, discreet, economical, honest, and most essentially, never idle."

Though Justine had hoped for something better, things were so bad with her that she felt she had little choice in the matter, and immediately accepted the situation and was installed the very same evening.

Mr. Hairpin was a very frugal man. He never used any light in his rooms but what came through the window from a street lamp just opposite. Linen of any kind, such as sheets, towels, napkins or tablecloths, he and his wife never knew the use of either—they thought it the maddest extravagance; and those that Justine made they carefully stowed away in some secret recess of the house as a treasure to be hidden from the eyes of men. And as for wine—it was never seen even on holiday festivals. Pure water, Madame Hairpin used to say, was the natural drink of man, the most wholesome and least pernicious.

His self-abnegation Mr. Hairpin almost carried to the point of a religious exaltation; and in his constant denying himself superfluities of any kind felt himself in the company of the great saints and anchorites of the past. Ever watchful, he never suffered a single lapse from his high ascetic ideal; and at meal-times whenever the bread was being cut he used to place a basket under the knife to catch the falling crumbs, which were conserved with great care until Sunday, when they were fried in a pan with butter. It was a great delicacy with them and their principal holiday meal. And their clothes and household stuffs, for fear of wearing them out, were never at any time cleaned, the inconvenience of which did not in the least give them any bother. And they lined with iron the soles of their shoes, which were the same ones they wore on their wedding day, thirty years ago.

In the lodging above them there lived a well-to-do man who was a jeweler by trade, and who possessed a large collection of fine jewels which Mr. Hairpin long had his eye on. Justine often heard him tell his wife of a certain gold box which he said he would like to get his hands on.

But Mr. Hairpin hated to mess with things of that sort and wished to entrust Justine with the business of getting this treasure.

"My dear Therese," he said to her one day, "stealing is one of the chief means of reestablishing an equilibrium of wealth. The poor can only better their condition by stealing from the rich, the rich increase their wealth by robbing the poor. It's a natural law. Besides, my dear, very few thefts are punished; there are countries in which it is even honored as a noble deed, and the thief rewarded for proving his courage, skill and nobility. You will not be caught, and if you do, I'll get you out of the scrape easily enough."

With this he handed her two keys, one for his neighbor's lodgings, and another for his small private vault, and pleaded with her to go at once and fetch him the treasure; and as a reward for her signal service he promised to give her another franc at the end of the year.

"Oh, sir!" cried Justine, "can it be that the master wishes to corrupt his servants so? Who will later stop me from turning against yourself the very same weapon you now put into my hand? Whom will you have to blame if one day I make you the victim of your own teachings?"

To conceal his confusion Mr. Hairpin fell back upon a clumsy subterfuge, and told her he was merely testing her honesty with his strange proposals, and that she was very lucky to have refused him.

14

But Justine paid heavily for answering so boldly, for with criminals one must either fully fall in with them or completely avoid them; and had she known that she might have been spared a great deal of unhappiness. But it must have been decreed in Heaven that for every honest impulse of hers she was to be paid off with a misfortune.

Mr. Hairpin did not give her much further trouble for some time. He seemed to ignore her completely. But it was about the end of her second year's service in his house that one night, after having gone to bed, her door was suddenly flung open and in rushed Mr. Hairpin clamoring wildly, with four policemen.

"There she is!.... that's her!... she's the crook who stole my diamonds! They must be hidden somewhere in this very room!"

"I!... robbed you!... good heavens! How can you accuse me of such a deed!"

Mr. Hairpin raised such a din that Justine's words could not be heard. The diamonds were soon found underneath the mattress where they were hidden by Mr. Hairpin himself; and Justine was immediately handcuffed and led off to the jail.

Her trial was speedily gotten over with, for she had neither money nor political influence to prove her innocence. No matter how well she might defend herself the odds were against her: a master was indicting a servant: the diamonds were found in her room: did she know anybody with connections!—it was evident she was a thief. And when she tried to tell the judge of Mr. Hairpin's proposal to rob his neighbor, which she refused, and thereby show that he was now accusing her through malice, the court looked upon her defense as outrageous recrimination. Mr. Hairpin was an upright and prosperous citizen, incapable of such a charge. And so, with little more ado she was convicted and hustled off to the prison cells.

Chapter 4

SHE WAS crowded into a small cell with three other women, with one of whom, a middle-aged woman called Madame Dubois, Justine immediately struck up a warm intimacy. In Madame Dubois Justine thought she found a kindred and sympathetic soul, which was the crying need of her suffering heart; and to this new companion of hers she was soon telling all her troubles. And it was many a long, tedious day they whiled away together in the most impassioned, tender confidences.

One evening Madame Dubois told her to be on the alert and not go to bed, that she had friends on the outside who were going to set fire to the jail that night. "Of course many prisoners will burn to death; but what do we care as long as we make our escape."

About eight the fire broke out. Twenty-one prisoners died in the fire. But Madame Dubois and Justine made a safe getaway, and with the help of four friends of Madame Dubois readied a poacher's hut in the Forest of Bondy that same night.

"There you are, Therese!" Madame Dubois cried, "free as a bird!—and you can do as you please! But listen to me and give up what you call virtue, which, as you see, never got you anywhere. An honest deed almost brought you to the gallows, a crime saved you from it. What use is good in the world, anyway? It's not worth sacrificing ourselves for it. You're young and pretty, Therese: in two years I can make a fortune for you. If you wish to get on in this world, dear girl, we must follow more than one trade, and serve more than one master. But you've got to make up your mind quick—we've got to get out of here soon!"

"Oh, Madame Dubois, I owe you a great deal! You have saved my life; although I should have preferred death myself to an act that brought death to others—alas, I was helpless! Now I feel the great danger I'm in; but oh, madame, still I prefer the thorns of virtue to the glittering favors of sin! Thank god that my principles of religion shall never leave me; and if they make my life painful in this world, I shall be rewarded for it in a better world to come! Such thoughts console me, sweeten my sorrows and strengthen my spirit in distress!"

"Bosh!" Madame Dubois said, "The justice of God!—his rewards! his punishments!—all nonsense! Don't you see that the cruelty of the rich forces the poor to rebel! Why don't they open their purses to our needs? Let humanity rule their hearts, then virtue will rule ours! Our misfortune, our patience, our faith, our servility only strengthen our fetters. We are all created free and equal by nature; but if chance puts out of order this first law of nature, is it not up to us to correct its caprices by our strength and numbers? Because we are poor, Therese, must we crawl in humiliation, must we quench our thirst with gall, must we satisfy our hunger with stones! Would you have us abstain from crime and murder, which alone can open the gates of life to us? As long as this class domineers over us we'll remain degraded, in want and tears! No! no! Therese, either your God is rich or impotent! Understand, my child, that if your God puts us in a situation where evil is necessary and at the same time gives us the ability to perform it, it is evident that your God gains as much from the one as the other!"

But the words of this crafty woman did not for a moment weaken the faith in Justine's heart; and her conscience easily refuted the sophisms of Madame Dubois. Justine declared that never would she allow herself to become corrupted or waver in her faith and principles. "Well, do as you please!" said Madame Dubois, "I leave you to your fate. But if you ever get hung, by that fatal irony which always rewards crime at the price of virtue, remember my words!"

All this while Madame Dubois' four comrades were drinking heavily with the poacher. No sooner had they heard Justine's resolution than they rose from the table and held a consultation with Madame Dubois, the proceedings of which made Justine tremble with fear. The upshot of it was the choice given her of either submitting to them willingly and getting paid for it, or being forced to submit and cruelly beaten for her pains. Justine threw herself at Madame Dubois' knees and begged her to save her again; but Madame Dubois laughed at her.

"Oh hell!" she said, "you sure are unfortunate!—what! you refuse such four able bodied men! Why, you little fool, there are ten thousand women in Paris who would give half their wealth to be in your place!" And after a little thought she added, "Listen! I'm boss here and I can save you—but only on one condition."

"Oh, madame, what must I do?" Justine wailed. "You must become one of us and do what we do without hesitation. Hesitation is death. Under this condition will I save you."

The threatening gestures of the men struck such fear into her that Justine readily assented and said, "I promise to obey you; only save me from the fury of these men!"

"Boys!" said Madame Dubois, "this girl is now one of us, and don't anyone dare touch her. Let us better get busy. Can't you realize that she may be useful to us? Let's use her for our interests, not for our pleasure."

But the wine had already gone to their heads and they could not be brought to submission and refused to listen to Madame Dubois. They devoured Justine with fiery looks and were ready to sacrifice her.

"Will it not be necessary to show proofs of her virtue? Will she not be of greater use to us as a maiden?" Madame Dubois, who wished to stay their fury, asked.

"Hold on!" cried one of the bandits, who looked like a bull, "hold on, my comrades! It is impossible to satisfy ourselves in the usual way. Since the little girl's virtue is so precious to her and ourselves she may keep it. But we must be satisfied some way—any way at all! Let Therese strip herself naked at once!"

"Strip myself naked!" Justine said. "Oh heavens! what do you want? If I give myself up to your looks wouldn't you....?"

The man was not in the mood to be delayed and got up and struck Justine brutally and compelled her to obey. He then propped her on his knees, and forcing her to lean over commenced striking her violently with the battering ram of his open hand. His first blows made her fall forward, but one of the other men held her by the shoulders to keep her firm in position for the blows, which she could not possibly avoid and were making her black and blue. "In her place I would have given myself up rather than be shattered in this way... harder! harder!" he exploded.

The second bandit beat her with his open palms across the cheeks, the mouth, the ears, the breasts, until the color in her skin turned purple-red. She begged for pity, tears flowing down her cheeks; but the sight of them only redoubled his blows.

And the third, a scatologomaniac, forced her to submit to his outlandish fancies.

The fourth fastened cords to every part of her body, and about six feet away from her held the other ends tightly in his hands. As Madame Dubois fondled and kissed him he pulled sharply on the cords, chuckling gleefully all the while. Justine staggered and fell every time he yanked at them; and finally he gave one terrific pull, so that Justine fell quite close to him, her forehead, bosom and cheeks bearing the marks of his delirium. Thus she suffered, but her virtue was preserved.

Satisfied, the bandits set out at once. The next night they slept under haycocks on the outskirts of Louvres. Justine had hoped to spend the night by the side of Madame

Dubois, but madame had other companions for the night, and so she was forced to sleep alone. Her trepidation was too intense to allow her any sleep, and she was still wide awake some hours later when the chief came up to her saying, "Sweet Therese, you will not deny me the happiness of spending the night near you?" And to reassure her he added, "Don't be afraid, we shall only talk and I'll do nothing against your will."

"Oh, Therese!" he continued, "is it not foolish to pretend with us you're so pure? If it wasn't for the interests of the gang do you think we'd have let you remain a virgin long? You know very well that we let you keep your charm simply to catch suckers."

"Oh God! oh God!... since you know that I prefer death to dishonor what use am I to you?"

"We can use you for our profit or our pleasure. Your misfortune forced this upon you. But you know, Therese, everything can be straightened in this world. Now listen to me, and make up your mind: give yourself to me, dear girl, to me alone, understand, and I'll save you from the sad life ahead of you."

"I, sir!" Justine cried, "I become the mistress of a...!"

"Come on, don't be afraid—say it! A robber, is it not? I admit that; but I can't offer you anything else. You're aware that people like myself never marry. Marriage is a sacrament, and all sacraments are hateful to us. But is it not better, my little one, to give yourself up to one man who will become your lover and protector than prostitute yourself with all?"

"But why must I do either?" she asked.

"Because right is with the strong, and you are weak. Besides, isn't it ridiculous for you to set so high a price on such a trifle! How can a girl be so simple to believe that virtue depends upon a little more or less skin! The intentions of nature are that all living creatures should perform

20

the duties they were designed for. And since woman was formed for man's enjoyment, it is criminal in the scheme of things for her to resist. This virtue of yours, my dear, then, far from serving nature, tends to hinder it. But never mind all this, dear girl. I only desire to please you, and will not take advantage of your weakness, and steal from you that which you value so highly. A woman has more than one favor to bestow upon a man; and I shall be content with the smallest one. Need I say more to you, Therese? We will find therein the needs for our happiness. Please try, Therese, please try and we shall be happy!"

"Oh, sir!" Justine replied, "I don't understand what it's all about; but if it's what I think it is, it is an outrage to womanhood! It most grievously offends nature and the hand of Heaven avenges it in this world!"

"What rot, my dear, what rot! Who taught you all this nonsense? If the seed of life is put in us for the sole purpose of propagation, I grant you then that the misplacing of it is an offense to nature. But if nature created the seed for other reasons, which is quite obvious, then what difference does it make if it is lost in one place or another. Moreover, the ability we have in misplacing the vital fluid proves conclusively that it does not offend nature. The limitation of offspring, the destruction of seed, Therese, are in the eyes of nature but imaginary crimes."

He found potent strength in his own words, which greatly fired his enthusiasm; and he wished that Justine learn more persuasively the truth of what he was saying. And she, though not blinded by the ardor of his reasonings, to preserve what was more valuable to her, was ready to yield, had they not just then heard the joltings of a carriage on the highway. He immediately quit his pleasure and turned to duty; and calling his men together, he rushed to fresh crimes. They shortly returned loaded with spoils, with blood on their hands.

"Let's beat it!" said Madame Dubois, "it's no longer safe here."

They divided the booty and gave Justine her share, which she dared not refuse; and then packed up and hurried away.

Next day they found themselves in the Forest of Chantilly, where they counted the money got by last night's holdup; which they did not find to be much.

"Well," one of them said, "it sure wasn't worth while bumping off these birds for so little!"

"Not so fast, old man, not so fast!" cried Madame Dubois. "It was me who told you to kill those guys—and for a good reason. Since murder and robbery are the same in the eyes of the law, why shouldn't we kill to cover up our job? We should never value things except how they concern ourselves. The death of these three guys meant nothing to us— sure you don't give a damn whether they be alive or dead. Therefore if we got the slightest gain doing away with them we ought to be glad. The only other feelings that may be involved are moral ones, and moral feelings are always false; the only real feelings worth bothering about are physical ones. The weakness of our bodies, lack of reason, the stupid prejudices in which we are brought up, the vain promises of religion, and the laws are what stop fools from becoming criminals and doing great deeds! But a man strong and vigorous knows where his interests really lie, and he mocks God and man, braves death, despises the laws and is thoroughly convinced that he alone is the measure of all things!"

"Oh, madame," cried Justine, "do you not feel the condemnation of Heaven written in your words? Your principles may be all right for a man powerful enough to fear nothing; but we who are outlaws, always in danger, ought we to recognize a system that only sharpens the sword hanging over our heads?-How can you expect him who struggles against the combined interest of all not to perish? Is not society united against him, and can he fight against all? Society is sustained by mutual exchanges of benefits; but your hero, instead of offering benefits, only offers crimes. Man will unite to destroy him at all cost! Even among ourselves, madame, how can you expect united effort when you counsel everyone to follow his own interests only! Shall you find fault with anyone of us who might murder his companion for money? What stronger argument for virtue need I give than proving the necessity of our keeping together!"

"What say you, sweet Therese," answered the leader, "is only apparently true. Virtue does not keep us together—only our selfish interests bind us. The reason that I, the strongest of the gang, do not murder my comrades is because I need their help. It is for the same reason that they do not stick a dagger into my back. Such a motive is a selfish one, though it has the appearance of virtue. What society calls its interest is nothing but a mass of private interests put together. If you have nothing to offer to society what interest does it take in you? The best thing such a man can do is to retire from society altogether, which is only interested in itself, and join those who struggle against its combined selfishness. So you see, man is really born isolated, selfish, cruel and despotic; he wants everything and gives nothing in return. And he will always fight and maintain his ambition and rights by legislation and blood. True, to stop this eternal bloodshed men yield a little to each other, forming what you call society. I find no fault with such an arrangement, but I firmly believe that the underdog should never submit to it, for society is an arrangement for the advantage of the rich and powerful only; the weak can find their sole reward in merely consoling themselves in their own way; for outcasts like ourselves there are only two means, crime or death!"

"Oh, sir!" replied Justine with vehemence, "if a man is reasonable will he not seek that eternal happiness assured by virtue? If I grant, for the sake of argument, that crime may make you momentarily happy here below, will not God take vengeance on you in the other world? Do not believe anything else!" She continued in tears, "Paradise is sufficient consolation for the unfortunate ones! You can't take that away from us! If men abandon us here God will avenge us!"

"Paradise, my sweet Therese, may console some, but it's the bunk. The poor must suffer! It is one of nature's laws. Their existence is necessary to create prosperity. This truth makes tyrants and exploiters possible. Nature wills it thus. When her secret workings make us do evil it is because evil is necessary to her scheme. Let no one be frightened or hindered if his soul forces him to evil. Let him commit crimes without regrets as soon as he feels the necessity! It is only by resisting such an urge that men act against nature. But let us not talk about nature, dear girl, since you insist on theology.—The primitive man, frightened by the natural phenomena about him, naturally thought that some unknown spirit was directing the thunder and lightning—it is natural for the weak to fear force. And so the mind of this child-man, unable to understand natural laws, created a gigantic being in his own image as ruler of the universe; and worshipped him as such. Every separate family invented such a being for themselves; and over the face of the earth there arose as many gods as families. Under these idols it is easy to see the first fruits of human blindness. True, they carved them differently, but it's always the same. Now, Therese, because idiots talk nonsense to wooden images must the wise man give up his joy in this world? Should he, like the dog in the fable, lose his bone because of an image? No, there is no God! Nature is sufficient in itself, and needs no creator. God, you see, presupposes a creation—a time when there was nothing, or when all was chaos. Now, if either of these states was bad why did your God permit it to exist; if it was good, why did he change it; if everything is now good

24

what else can your God do; if he is useless can he be powerful; if nature moves by itself, what use the mover? Observe how these contradictory reasons destroy one another! You must admit that this *Phantom* sprung from ignorance and fear. It is utter nonsense which deserves neither belief nor a minute's examination from an intelligent person! It is a stupid extravagance hateful to the mind and revolting to the heart; and must return to the darkness whence it sprung!"

Justine was ready to refute these blasphemous reasonings, but the sound of a horse's hoofs reached their ears.

"To arms!" cried the chief.

They were off. They soon brought back an unlucky traveler whose name the robbers learned was Florent; and that he was a business man from Lyons on his way home.

He offered them all the money he had with him in payment for his safety. It was a large sum, and the bandits seemed well satisfied. But, nevertheless, the chief said, holding a gun under the man's nose, "Friend, you know very well that we can't let you live!"

Just then Justine rushed forward and, throwing herself at the feet of the chief, cried, "Sir, I beg you to spare his life— do me this one favor, please!" And suddenly thinking of an idea that might help save the man's life she continued, now addressing their captive, "Florent? Why, I believe that we are related to one another. But do not be so surprised to find one of your relatives in the position you find her. I'll explain everything later." Then turning to the chief again she added, "Spare this man's life and in return I shall do anything you ask." The chief answered, "You know what I want, sweet Therese!"

"Ah, good sir, I shall do anything—yes, anything!" she cried.

"Let him live!" commanded the chief. "But he must become one of us!"

Rather than be shot the merchant only too readily consented to join them. They gave him food and drink and later went off to sleep.

But the chief came back to Justine and said, "I expect you to keep your promise, though I'm too tired tonight. You better lie down with Dubois. I expect you about daybreak; if you refuse me then it'll be too bad for you and that cousin of yours!"

"Happy dreams to you!" answered Justine. "I want nothing better than keep my promise!"

But it was many hours, after much tippling, before the men sprawled all over the ground and fell asleep, dead drunk; Madame Dubois, in whose care they left Justine, was drunk like the rest.

The harsh and heavy snoring of the sleepers, stretched out insensible to right and left of her, reassured Justine that it was quite safe to go to their newly taken prisoner and have a few words with him.

"Sir," she whispered to him quietly, "I, too, am a prisoner here, I loathe them all. I am no relative of yours—I just said that to save you. Let us run away together—now is the time! You see that I place myself in your hands. Pity my unfortunate lot and show respect to my honor, which I trust to you; it is the only thing I possess!"

Florent expressed his gratitude in lavish terms, but they had little time for talking.

Justine cleverly recovered Florent's wallet, returned it to him, and then they both speedily cleared into the underwood and made for a path, that led out of the forest. By daybreak they safely reached a small town, where they rested without any fear.

From his manner and speech Florent seemed to be a man of great tenderness. He told Justine that he would fulfill all her hopes. "All I ask," he said, "is to repay the kindness you showed me. I owe you my fortune, Therese," he added, kissing her hands, "and also my life. Can I do more than offer you both. Accept them, I beg you; let our marriage bind closer the knot of our friendship!"

Justine could not withhold an expression of surprise and refusal on her face, which he noticed; and so he limited himself to just asking what he could do for her.

"Sir," Justine answered, "if you are really sincere in what you say, all I would want of you is to take me with you to Lyons and get me a place in some respectable home where my honor and virtue would not be in such danger."

"Fine! fine!" cried Florent, "I'll surely be able to place you!"

The young merchant then asked her why she left Paris, the city of her birth; whereupon she told him all her past misfortunes, and how at present she was a fugitive from justice.

"Oh, if it is only that," he said, "I can be of use to you before we reach Lyons. You need no longer fear the authorities; they will never look for you in the home I'm going to place you. I know a woman in the country who'll gladly accept you; I'll introduce you to her tomorrow."

The rest of the day they remained in town. Next morning after an early breakfast they started out on foot; it was fine weather and but a few miles to their destination.

"We have all day ahead of us, let's take our time," said Florent, who was growing more and more amiable. And again he spoke of how much he was beholden to her arid the great desire he had to repay her for all she had done for him.

Towards noon they left the open highway and took a short cut across an open field leading into a dense cover of woods, which but for a random ray here and there slipping through the black-green foliage, almost completely blotted out the sun beating down over their heads.

There was profound silence and isolation all around, which the fitful calls of birds made even more intense. But Justine, nevertheless, felt very much at ease and reassured. Florent was extremely considerate and courteous; moreover, she had grown so used to his company that she forgot its very existence; arid fascinated by the romantic gloom of the place she was quite carefree and heedless.

They were walking along a small footpath, Justine a little ahead of Florent, when she turned round and asked if they still had far to go.

"No, whore!" he cried, and knocked her to the ground with a blow from his cane, where she lay unconscious....

When she regained her senses she found herself lying at the foot of a tree, benumbed, smeared with blood and dishonored. Bewildered, honorless, hopeless, she wished she were dead.

"The monster!" she said, "what have I done to him to deserve such evil treatment! I gave him his life, returned his money to him; and in return he stole from me what I held most precious and dear. Oh, men! when you listen only to your passions wolves in the wastes of Russia hold you in contempt!"

Her eyes, full of tears, instinctively turned toward Heaven, and her heart went out to the Great Master residing there; and she fell upon her knees and prayed to Him: "Holy and Majestic Being, in this awful moment you fill my soul with Heavenly Joy! Oh, my Protector and Guide, I aspire to Your Goodness, and implore Your Clemency! Behold my woes and sorrows! Oh, Mighty God, you know that I am innocent! I was betrayed when I wished only to do good after Your Commandments! You will punish him for it, oh, my God!"

Prayer is the sweetest consolation of the unhappy, and she rose full of courage, gathered her clothes together and hid behind a thick growth of bushes. But she was very weak and exhausted, and could walk no farther; and so she lay down, wearily closed her eyes and fell into a profound sleep.

Chapter 5

IT WAS next day, the sun high in the sky, when Justine awoke. The moment of awakening is most terrible to the unfortunate; the imagination, refreshed and strengthened by the sweetness of sleep, quickly fills the soul with sorrowful remembrances.

"Is it worth while to be born to such a life?" she said, her tears flowing freely. And hardly had she wiped them away when she heard a noise near her, and saw two men just outside of the bush behind which she was concealed. "Come, dear," said one of them, "we are pretty safe here. My detestable aunt will not hinder us now in our sweet pleasures!"

Justine was very curious and did not avoid seeing their actions; and right before her eyes she was witness to a scene which she found very singular, and could not make out. One of the men who lent himself to the business was about twenty-four, and of aristocratic appearance. The other seemed to be one of his servants.

At last they were about to return home. The master by chance approached the bush which hid Justine and espied her bonnet.

"Jasmine!" he quickly called to his footman, "we are discovered! a girl has witnessed our mysteries!—Come out, you strumpet, and be quick about it.!"

Justine came out trembling, and fell upon her knees before them.

"Oh, gentlemen," she cried, "take pity on a miserable, unfortunate girl!"

But Count Bressac, into whose hands she had fallen, was a man little given to sentiments of pity; what is more, he had a pronounced disgust for the female sex. "You blockhead!" he bellowed at her. "If you hope to find us easy, have another guess! We have damn little use for you and it's pity you expect, huh? But speak, you dumb ass, what have you seen around here?"

"I heard you talking on the grass, nothing else," she said.

"All right, I'll believe you; if I thought you saw anything else you'd never leave here alive!—Jasmine, it is early yet. We'll hear first what the girl has to say for herself, and then decide what to do after."

The young men sat down, placed Justine near them and had her relate all the misfortunes befallen her ever since her sorry entrance into this very sad, terrible world. When she told all she had to say, Count Bressac said, "Come, Jasmine, let's get rid of her—she's a nuisance. Let's kill her, what d'you say?"

They dragged her behind the bushes, laughing at her tears, to a very small clearing skirted by a luxuriant growth of saplings.

"Let's tie her hands and feet in the form of a square, to these four trees here," said Count Bressac.

Out of their shirts, neckties and handkerchiefs they soon made enough rope to bind her in the most painful manner possible. It seemed to her that her belly, weighted down toward the ground, would rip open any minute; and she thought they were tearing her legs apart. She felt alive only through the violence of her pain. But both men were tickled by her posture and suffering, and hugged and amused each other while watching her.

"That's enough," the Count said at last, "I'll let her get away with it this time.—Therese," he continued, loosening her, "if you are discreet and do as I tell you, you will not regret it. My aunt needs a woman to help her in the house. I'll recommend you to her; but I'll be responsible for your behavior. Remember, if you abuse my kindness or betray me, or refuse to submit to my will—think of these four trees!"

She immediately forgot her pains and threw herself at the

Count's feet and swore through her tears that she would always obey him.

"All right," he said, "let's go; it's your good conduct that will decide your future."

She followed them in humble silence, Jasmine and his master often whispering together. In less than an hour they arrived at Count Bressac's castle, where Justine was ushered into a small room and told to wait until they came back for her. Jasmine soon brought back something for her to eat. The young Count also shortly returned; and took Justine with him and presented her to Countess Bressac, his aunt.

Countess Bressac, a woman in her late forties, was a kind, simple person. Her husband, the young Count's uncle, had died some time ago, and Count Bressac's income depended on his aunt's liberality; what his father gave him was not enough to keep up this fine house, or even cover the expense of his pleasures.

Three months in the year the Countess spent in her nephew's house; the rest of the year she lived in Paris. These three months he considered an affliction, which he put up with only for the sake of her money.

When the Countess heard all Justine's troubles, she said to her, "I am sorry to hear of your misfortunes, and believe what you tell me. I will only verify the fact that you are the daughter of the man you mention, whom I knew as a big banker in Paris; which is another reason I take an interest in you. As for your former master, Mr. Hairpin, I'll settle him as soon as I get back to Paris. It will be easy for me to prove your innocence to my old friend, the Chancellor; he'll do anything I ask. But, Therese, I will do what I promise you only on condition you're telling me the truth."

Justine thanked her warmly. She was made a chambermaid.

In three days the inquiries the Countess made in Paris arrived, verifying Justine's story. The Countess was pleased to learn the truth. All fear of further misfortune now vanished from Justine's mind.

Chapter 6

COUNT BRESSAC was a very handsome man, whose waist and features belied his real sex. But what a soul he hid under those feminine charms; he was mean, cruel and contemptuous of any impulse of kindliness. Nevertheless, after becoming familiar with him Justine found it impossible to dislike him. Indeed, she felt a tenderness toward him that nothing seemed to be able to overcome. Notwithstanding her knowledge of his cruelty, his aversion for women, his peculiar, irregular tastes, she could not resist her awakening of passion for him. If he had demanded her life she would have sacrificed it a thousand times for his sake. But he never suspected her love for him, or discovered the cause of her daily tears; though the readiness with which she anticipated his wishes should have given him an inkling to her feelings. However, her behavior toward him at least won his confidence; and even for this small trifle she was extremely thankful.

Sometimes Justine took the liberty of mildly reprimanding him for his excesses, which were greatly impairing his health. He listened to her tolerably and ended by telling her that nobody ever corrected himself of a vice such as his.

"Ah, Therese!" he cried enthusiastically, "if you but knew the sheer joy we have in the sweet illusion of being no longer a man, but a woman! Happy contradiction of the mind: we abhor the sex and yet we imitate it! Ah, Therese, how sweet and delightful it is to be the wanton of all those who desire you! What delirium! what joy! To be on the very same day the mistress of a porter, a marquis, a valet, a duke! To be caressed, threatened, browbeaten and grown jealous of! Now in their victorious arms, now a victim of the fete— soothing them—reinflaming them! Oh, no, no! Therese, you can't understand this pleasure! Laying aside the moral, if you could only imagine the physical sensations of these divine practices!—It is impossible to resist them! It is a pleasure so keen, a titillation so quick and sharp... one loses his wits, talks nonsense.... I A thousand kisses, one more tender than another.... Rolled up in the lover's arms, mouth to mouth, we swoon into one being! If we ever complain, it is only of being neglected. We like our lovers to be more robust than Hercules. Do not imagine, Therese, that we are like other men; we are quite differently constructed. We are truly like women; and there is not a single pleasure known to you which is unknown to ourselves. So you see, this enchanted love of ours makes the correction of our tastes impossible; it would turn us into madmen if our pleasures were restrained!"

The Countess Bressac was not unacquainted with her nephew's riotous mode of life, and did everything possible to bring him into the path of virtue. But she did so with a little too much rigor. To spite her, he gave himself up to his debauches with greater abandon; and for her troubles the Countess got in return only greater abhorrence. To increase her misery he surrounded her only with servants who served his passions; he even went so far as to declare that if she interfered with his pleasures he would convince her of their charm before her very eyes.

She often gave way to tears; but her wretchedness gave him great satisfaction; and whenever Justine mentioned to him the sorrows his disorders caused his aunt he became impatient and angry.

"Do not imagine," he often said to her, "that my aunt is good to you of her own accord. Know that if I did not remind her all the time, she would hardly remember the promises she made you. She boasts a great deal about what she has done for you; whereas it is but my work. Yes, Therese, it is to me alone that you owe your gratitude. No matter how pretty you may be, you are aware I do not seek your favors; no, Therese, what I expect from you is something quite different. When you are convinced that it's me who has done you all the good, I expect you'll follow my wishes."

The cause of his violent hatred for his aunt Justine found hard to understand; the more she thought it over, the more was she puzzled; and to these vague, ominous hints of his she had no idea how to reply, and did so at random with too much apparent evasion. But she thought she might bring him around by imparting to him the sweetness of virtue. However, let alone be converted, the Count, a fervent enemy of philosophical mysteries, a stubborn stickler for anything militating against all dogma, and a raging antagonist against the existence of good, tried to corrupt her ardent faith.

"Therese," he said, "all virtue is born from a false principle. If the laws controlling nature, from which all her actions and reactions spring, require a necessary first essence, what later becomes of this sovereign thing? What is virtue if it cannot prevent the tyranny of the strong over the weak, or the rich over the poor, or those who are in power over those who are not in power! Filled with the will for power, the voices of virtue forge irons in which to chain men. And men, stupefied by their misery, willingly believe everything told them. Can virtue, sprung from such motives, win our respect? Is there a single truth which does not bear the mark of falsehood and lies? What do we find in them: mysteries that cause reason to shudder; dogmas that outrage nature; and ceremonies that inspire only disgust and derision!

"Can any man, no matter how virtuous change the face of the earth; can he destroy the plagues that afflict it; can he curb the viciousness that makes it foul; are we any more happy? Then what do the pretenders do? Through jugglers' tricks and puns some man announces himself to the world. And to whom?—only to menials and slaves and sluts this would-be ruler manifests his greatness: through drinking with one, sleeping with another he forces the hardened sinners to submit to his will; through inventions and farces, satisfying his lust and gluttony the scoundrel proves his mission. He makes his fortune, all right! Of course, you can always find a lot of scoundrels to join a rogue and form a sect. And so, soon the nonsense of this riffraff wins over a few fanatics: and before long fanaticism seizes the mind of the rabble; women bawl; fools beat themselves; idiots believe; and lo, the most despicable creature, the most awkward lout, the worst charlatan that has ever appeared in history—behold him- a leader—behold him a paragon of virtue! Behold all his ravings consecrated, all his lies become holy dogmas, all his idiotic tricks, mysteries!

"Even the so-called intellectuals believe his pronouncements. Since *he* said so, it must be so. If there were real virtue in the world, as you say there is, would it survive upon such absurd means; would it be through the mouth of such rascals that it would show itself? Could not the mover of the stars in heaven influence men's hearts itself; could it not engrave in the center of heaven the laws that would please all men from one corner of the earth to the other? Would your precious virtue indicate his desires only to this idol of yours, this vilest menial and craftiest rogue living in an ignored corner of Asia? No, Therese, I would rather die a thousand times than fall for such tripe!"

"Oh, sir!" Justine replied, "would you deprive an unfortunate girl of her one sweet hope; would you crush within her heart her one consolation? I firmly believe that blows levelled at virtue are mostly due to the effects of lust and dissipation. How can I sacrifice the dearest flower of my mind, the dearest pearl of my heart to such blasphemies, to such horrible sophisms?"

And to this she added many other protests. But the Count only laughed at her; and with vehement eloquence, borrowed from pamphlets that Justine happily never read, he constantly attacked her beliefs; but which, for all that, he never really succeeded in undermining.

In spite of his incorrigible opinions Justine was badly smitten with love for the Count, and often tried to kill the passion for him that was growing in her soul. But is it love and evil that can be cured? Every reason she found to oppose to it only fanned its flame the more; the more cause she found to hate him, the more charming he appeared to her.

Chapter 7

FIVE YEARS sped very quickly by. They were very happy years for Justine, who was still in the Countess' service. The Countess was a virtuous and pious woman whose goodness bound Justine to her forever. The nine months in the year they spent in Paris were especially pleasant. True, the other three months at Count Bressac's country estate were spoiled by the shadow his dissipations and mad pranks cast upon their happiness; but then she was near the man she loved, could breathe the very same air he did, and watch him come and go.

It was late in summer and Justine and her mistress were still staying at the Count's country seat.

Count Bressac did not as yet push forward certain schemes he had long been brewing against his aunt; though of late he had thrown out several vague hints to Justine, whose good will won from him many a private confession. He had complete confidence in her loyalty to him, to him alone.

One evening shortly after she had gone to bed he opened the door to her room and asked her to let him talk to her. Every minute of his time that he gave her Justine found too precious to refuse. He entered, carefully closed the door behind him and sat down next to her on the edge of the bed.

"Listen, Therese," he said with some embarrassment, "I have something very important to tell you. Swear that you will never reveal my secret."

"Sir/' she said, appearing hurt, "how can you believe that I would abuse any of your confidences?"

"Oh, you don't know the risk you run if I find I'm mistaken in you!"

"The worst of my sorrows would be to lose your trust—I need no other threats!"

"Well, Therese, it's this: I had long ago decided that my aunt must die; and you must help me."

"I help you!" she gasped, pulling her head back with stunned surprise. "Oh, sir, how can you think of such a thing! No, no! kill me if you want to, but don't ask me to do that!"

"Listen, Therese, I am not surprised at your refusal. But I can't see anything wrong with my intentions. Of course, in this case two objections present themselves to your unphilosophic eyes: the first is the murder of a fellow creature; and the second the evil involved. But be assured, dear girl, that worrying seriously about the crime involved in destroying someone like ourselves is nothing but foolishness. For the power of destroying matter is not granted to man; the most he can do is but vary its forms. And since every form is equal in the eyes of nature nothing is lost in changing them. Change continues her power and maintains her kinetic energy... Ah! what does it matter to her ever-creating womb if today matter is flesh and tomorrow worms! Can anybody say that the construction of a biped costs nature more than that of a little worm? If you can prove to me that nature's laws are upset by any such transmutation, then I will believe that murder is a crime. But when my studies have shown me that everything growing on the surface of this globe is equal in the eyes of nature, I can't convince myself that the changing of one of these into a thousand others is at all criminal.

All animals, all fish, all plants, all vegetation nourish themselves, destroy themselves, reproduce themselves in the same way; never really dying; only transforming themselves into different species. Since decomposition is necessary to nature's schemes, he who assists her in it, though this act be styled criminal, is actually in accord with her laws. Oh, Therese, it is man's vanity that says murder is a crime. This vain creature, believing himself the sublimest on earth, established the false principle that destroying him is infamous; and his most ardent desire is to be rid of that which lowers him. But his vanity does not alter nature. And if such ideas come to us from nature itself, can they possibly be unnatural? The passions are some of the means nature uses to accomplish her designs. Does she need individuals: she inspires love to continue the propagation of the species. Is destruction necessary to her: she plants in us lust, ambition, hatred, murder. But she does not at all give us the power to commit crimes that would disturb her economy. Would she create us were we able to act against her? If murder were not necessary to her scheme would she permit it? How can she be offended in seeing man do what she herself does every day? If she can only produce by means of destruction, *is* it not in harmony with her that we do likewise? Consequently, the most perfect being is the one whose activity causes the most change. The inactive being, that is, the virtuous one, since he seeks only tranquillity, would soon plunge everything into chaos if allowed his own way. Equilibrium must be conserved; and this can only be realized through change, that is, *crime!"*

"But the person you wish to do away with is your own aunt!" Justine pleaded.

"Such arguments are frivolous in the eyes of a philosopher! I will not speak to you about it again—it is useless. Can such weak ties, the fruit of our gregarious instinct, hold a distinction in your eyes! Put aside your scruples, Therese, and serve me; your fortune will be made."

"Oh, sir," she cried, terrified, "the indifference you find in nature is only the result of your own way of looking at it; but listen to your heart and hear how it condemns your false reasonings. And is not the heart also created by nature; and if she engraves therein a deep horror of what you plan, is it not because she believes it criminal? Your passions blind your reason at present. If you commit the murder, tomorrow remorse will torture you. Oh, sir, respect the last days of your dear friend, your aunt, and do not sacrifice her to your passions! Every day, everywhere, you will see her image before you; you'll hear her sad voice calling the names of those who gave you joy in your childhood. She will disturb your waking hours and torment you in your sleep. She'll open with her ashy fingers the wounds you inflicted upon her; you'll not find a happy moment thereafter; and a heavenly hand whose power you forget will avenge the deed!" She fell upon her knees and with tears begged him by everything he held sacred to forget his wicked plans. And she swore that all her life she would conceal what he intended to do.

But he rose coolly and said, "I clearly see now that I was mistaken in you; I feel sorry for you. I shall find someone else. But you'll suffer anyway, without gaining anything for your mistress."

This overt threat changed all Justine's ideas immediately; and after some deliberation with herself she pretended to consent to his wishes. But as a subterfuge, to cover up her confusion and the suddenness with which she changed her mind, she asked him to repeat his arguments. Little by little, she seemed to yield to the force of his logic; and the Count really believed that she was finally being won over by his reasonings. At last she completely fell in with his ideas; and in his joy he embraced her.

"You are the first woman I ever kissed," he said. "You are

a delightful child. Wisdom finally penetrated your mind; is it possible this charming head could have remained in the darkness so long?"

He carefully outlined to her his whole scheme. In two or three days, at her first opportunity, she was to slip some poison into a cup of chocolate, which the Countess drank every morning on rising. And he promised her two thousand francs the very day she carried it out.

Two days after this last interview the Count learned that an uncle of his had died and left him a large inheritance.

On hearing the news Justine said to herself, "Oh, God! is this how you punish a criminal?" But immediately repenting this blasphemy, she fell upon her knees and asked forgiveness; for on second thought she was happy because she felt this unexpected event would change the Count's intent. However, she was mistaken.

That night he came running into her room and cried, "Oh, Therese, how lucky I am! I've often told you that crime was the only way to win happiness."

"Sir," said Justine, "I hope this unexpected windfall will now influence you to await the natural death of your dear aunt."

"Await!" he quickly replied. "Where did you get that idea from? You forget I am already twenty-nine, and am growing old! No, we'll change nothing in our plans—tomorrow; the day after tomorrow at latest!"

It was a great effort for her to conceal her true feelings. She was sure that if she did not carry out the crime in a day or two the Count would become suspicious of her real intentions. But if she warned Countess Bressac, no matter what action she would take, the Count, finding himself deceived, would speedily kill them both. Nevertheless, she finally decided to put the Countess on her guard; and next day she said to her, "Madame, I have something very important to reveal to you; but I'll remain silent unless you promise that you will not hurt the parties involved. You will act, madame, I am sure, honorably; but you must not say a word."

The Countess thought it concerned one of her nephew's follies; and swore to Justine to do as she wished.

Justine then revealed everything to her.

"The monster!" the Countess cried, "what have I ever done to him to deserve his hatred? If I corrected him now and then, it was only with the thought of his own happiness. Does he not owe to my influence over my brother the wealth he just inherited! I can't believe it! You must prove it to me!"

Justine showed her the small bottle of poison which the Count had given her; the Countess was no longer in doubt. They tried some on one of the dogs. The poor animal died soon after in terrible convulsions, so strong was the poison's virulence.

In a blind rage the Countess sent a message to one of her cousins in Paris, asking him to go to the Minister and speak to him about taking measures against her nephew; she also begged him to come and deliver her from the scoundrel's hands. But the message was put in the hands of a servant who, unbeknown to the Countess, was one of the Count's lovers; and he, suspecting something amiss, relayed the message to the Count, who went off to his room with rage in his heart.

When he met Justine he smiled to her as usual and said, "Therese, I found a safer way of doing the thing, but it will require long instructions. You'll meet me at the corner of the park at seven tonight, and we'll take a little walk during which I shall explain everything to you." Justine, never suspecting his discovery of her secret arrangements with the Countess, promised she would meet him; for in spite of everything, she was always secretly happy in his company. And then again, she thought there was still some hope left of dissuading him from carrying out his designs.

At the appointed time and place Justine was waiting for him impatiently; and when, almost an hour later, she saw him in the distance slowly approaching her, she felt her heart beat fast. He came up with a gay and easy smile and greeted her pleasantly.

She never saw him in so pleasant a mood; and they walked for some time, laughing and jollying each other with little pleasantries. Whenever Justine nervously turned the conversation to the business on hand he good-naturedly told her to wait.

She soon forgot everything, except that they were alone together, he close at her side, and that thick clusters of stars were shining overhead, that the country was beautiful on a night like this. And a happiness sharp as pain brought tears to her eyes.

Lost in her dreams, she finally found herself with him at the same four trees where, five years before, she had suffered so much agony at his hands. It immediately brought back to her mind all the terror of her former experience, and she drew back with fright. From one of the trees some ropes were already dangling, and to one of the other trees three huge mastiffs were securely tied, their mouths frothing and gaping hideously.

The Count abruptly turned to her and said in a somewhat vulgar tone, "Bitch! do you recognize this bush from which I dragged you like a beast, and gave you your life when you really should have been murdered? Do you recognize these trees where I promised to replace you if you did not behave? You whore, why did you accept my proposals if you intended to betray me? How did you expect to serve virtue by betraying him who helped you! Placed between two crimes, why did you choose the worse? You should have refused, you slut!" Digging his nails into her, he continued, "What have you accomplished betraying me? You have only risked your own life without saving my aunt's; she's been dead more than an hour already. You, too, must die! But before dying you must learn that the path of virtue is not the safest!"

And giving her no time to reply he dragged her mercilessly to the tree from which the ropes were hanging limp, and where one of his servants, eager and impatient, was waiting for him.

"Here she is!" the Count said. "She wanted to poison my aunt! I really should have given her into the hands of justice."

They tied her to the tree with a rope wound round her legs, but leaving her arms free so that she could fight off the dogs. The Count, much amused by the expression of terror on her face, walked round her, pinching her. "Tender!—fine breakfast for my dogs!" he said. And then he cried to his assistant, "All set?—let them loose!"

The dogs were unchained, and the Count sicked them on. They rushed upon Justine in a mad, snarling rage. She vainly tried to hold them off, but they bit into her with only greater fury. But the Count, for some secret motive of his own, soon called them off; otherwise they would have torn Justine to shreds.

"Well, that's enough," he said. "Chain the dogs; let's leave the slut to her fate." And untying her, he cooingly said, "Well, Therese, virtue is an expensive luxury, as you see. Don't you think that two thousand dollars are worth more than the bites you're covered with?"

The pain Justine felt submerged his words and she fell at the foot of the tree unconscious.

When she came to her senses again he ordered her to pick herself up and dress and leave the place at once. She gathered her floating wits together, and pulled up some grass to wipe the clots of blood from her body. The swelling of her flesh, the loss of blood and the excruciating pain she felt, all compelled her to dress very slowly. Meanwhile, Bressac walked back and forth occupied with his own thoughts.

Then he said to her, "Go wherever you like. You still must have some money about you; I'll not take it from you. But be sure you never cross my path again! The whole world will know that you poisoned my aunt! That is the only reason I let you leave here alive."

"Oh, sir!" she replied, "no matter how cruelly you've treated me, you need not fear that I will expose you. I believed it my duty to take some measures against you when it was a question of your aunt's life; but I shall never undertake any when I, myself, am personally concerned. Good-bye, may your crimes make you as happy as your cruelties have made me suffer. I shall always pray for you. Good-bye!"

Left to her sorrows, Justine fell down at the foot of a tree and gave full vent to her anguish. She pressed her bleeding body to the ground and washed the grass with her tears. "Oh, my God!" she wept, "it is Your eternal decrees that the innocent shall become the prey of the guilty; so be it! Make me suffer as You have suffered, O Lord! Make me worthy of the reward You promised to the meek! You are the joy of my tribulation, and the glory in my trials; O my Lord!"

Chapter 8

LATE NEXT day, hardly knowing how, she reached Marcel, a small town about ten miles out of Paris. There she inquired for a doctor, whom she told some fictitious story about being attacked at night by bandits who set their dogs on her. Doctor Rodin carefully examined her wounds, but found nothing really serious; and he told her that he could cure her in a few weeks if she remained in his house under his personal care. But Justine said she had only a little money. The doctor, however, generously declined to take any fees from her and said that in such a case, where it was more a question of humanity than money, he would gladly give her his services gratis. She was immediately put to bed, for she had a little fever.

In about three weeks Justine was well again. When she expressed a wish to enter some service in town until her funds permitted her to go farther, Doctor Rodin kindly offered her a place in his own home.

Doctor Rodin was a widower, and lived in a very large house with his daughter and two private maids. His daughter, Rosalie, was a small slip of a girl no more than fifteen, very delicate, but pretty. The two maids were also very pretty, which gave Justine pause to wonder. What use had he for a third maid and why all so young and pretty?

Doctor Rodin kept a charitable school in his house for young girls and boys, whom he never accepted under the age of twelve, and always dismissed when they arrived at sixteen. He himself taught the pupils. Justine expressed to Rosalie her surprise that the latter's father acted both as surgeon and teacher, and found it strange that such a wealthy man worked so hard. At these remarks Rosalie burst out laughing; and when Justine asked what was so funny in her remarks she said, "You're an innocent—that I see. But if you keep my secret I'll put you wise to everything. It is true that my father can get along without working so hard. He follows medicine as a hobby, for the sole pleasure of making fresh discoveries. He is well known in medical circles and is considered one of the best surgeons in France. But do you want to know why he keeps this school, Therese? Passion—passion...! Let me see... today is Friday, isn't it? Yes, today is the day, one of the three days in the week he corrects the pupils' mistakes. It's this exercise gives him such pleasure. Come with me and I'll show you what he does. We can see everything through a hole in the wall of my room, which is right next to his classroom. But we must be careful not to make any noise."

They were hardly in a safe position to spy on his doings

when they saw a young girl in tears followed into the empty classroom by Rodin. She was begging forgiveness.

"Oh, no! no!" cried Rodin, "I have forgiven you too often, Julie! I regret my kindness; it only makes you behave worse. What! you give notes to boys, do you!"

"I didn't! I didn't!"

"But I saw you—don't lie!"

At this point Rosalie said to Justine, "He is lying, not she! He only invents these things to find some reason for inflicting punishment upon them. This little girl is an angel."

Rodin seized the defenseless girl by the hands and tied them to a ring of a post standing in the center of the correction room. Julie turned her pretty head wistfully toward her tormentor, her tears flowing freely; but he gazed steadily upon this picture of misery and seemed to be enraged by it. Soon he could no longer refrain his fury and lashed her severely with a leather whip. The child shrieked terribly, but that only started fresh tyrannies in him. When he at last tired, he said to her, "All right now, but don't let it happen again. Next time I'll not be so lenient with you."

He led his pupil out of the room, but soon returned with a young boy about fifteen, whom he was scolding vehemently. "What! you little rascal, you mock me behind my back! I'll teach you!"

He flogged nine children, one right after another. "Oh heavens!" Justine said to Rosalie, "how can anyone abandon himself to such lust! How can anyone find pleasure in another's torments!"

"That's nothing!" replied Rosalie. "What you have just seen explains why my father runs a charitable school. But he does not stop there!"

In due time Justine learned that Rodin was also in the habit of scourging his daughter and the two maids, and that she, too, as a member of the household, was not to escape the pleasure he took in his cruelties.

Two days after the foregoing events he surprised her in bed. He pretended to have come to examine her wounds, and she could not resist his intrusion.

"Therese," he said, "you are completely cured. You can repay me very easily. This—is all I want, nothing more. You will, won't you?"

"Sir, how can I convince you that nothing in this world will entice me to do as you want. My gratitude to you is deep, but I can't pay you off by committing abominable crimes. This is all the money I have, take it and let me quit your house."

Doctor Rodin was much surprised at this refusal coming from a girl both homeless and penniless. He thought she would gladly do anything that cost no money.

"Therese!" he said, looking at her attentively, "it is wrong of you to play the virgin with me. I have some right to your complacency. But never mind. Keep your money and do not leave. I am glad to find an honest girl in my house; the others are anything but that. Since you are so virtuous, I hope you will always remain so. My daughter, Rosalie, is very fond of you; she would be heartbroken if you left us. Please do not leave, for her sake."

"But, sir," said Justine, "I will not be happy here. The other two women who wait on you will most likely become jealous of me, and I'll be forced to leave sooner or later."

"Never mind these women," Rodin reassured her, "I know how to keep them in their place. All I ask from you is discretion. Many things go on here that may shock you; but you will see everything and say nothing."

It was mostly the thought of Rosalie, who pleaded with her never to leave her, that prompted Justine's decision in staying.

A few days later Rodin said to her, "Therese, you will wait on my daughter; in that way you will not interfere with my other two women. I will pay you five hundred a year." She was highly pleased, and was beginning to think there was some good in the man. She soon dreamed of converting him. Before long she had a long conversation with him about good and evil.

"Do not imagine, Therese," he replied to her pious words, "that the kindness I have shown you is because I esteem virtue above vice. Do not imagine it. You would only deceive yourself. In a thoroughly vicious society virtue would be quite useless. But ours not being so, to weaken those who follow it, it is either necessary to take advantage of virtue or destroy it altogether. If nobody adopted it it would be useless. I'm not wrong, therefore, if I say that it exists only through opinion or accident. Virtue is not an absolute entity. It is nothing but a rule for conducting oneself, varying with each climate. Consequently, it is not real. This fact alone should prove its worthlessness. That only which is real and permanent is truly good. That which perpetually changes cannot be good. There are not two nations on the face of the earth whose virtues are the same. Since virtue is not real, not good, it does not deserve our esteem. We adopt it as a support in order that those who practice it may leave us in peace. How can you convince me that a virtue which suppresses natural emotions is good. Since the emotions are conflicting, some preferring vice, others virtue, which should we prefer? The only ones to be preferred, of course, are the ones that serve the individual best, both physically and mentally. If my hypothesis is true, some vices are very useful. You are told that virtue does good to others. In this sense, virtue would be useful if we admit that doing good to others is a good. For then in my turn I shall receive only good. This is mere sophistry. For the little good I receive from others by their practicing virtue I would be obliged to practice the same in turn. In this way I would make a million sacrifices, since the odds are a million to one, without receiving much in return. Receiving less than

I give is bad business. Would it not be wiser to refuse this mutual exchange of virtue which cost me so dear? But now I come, Therese, to the wrong I can do others and the evil I would receive in return, if everybody were like me. In admitting a whole society of vice, I run, it is true, the risk of receiving evil; but at the same time I am compensated by the pleasure of making others run the same risk. And so an equality is established in which everybody is happy. This could not exist in a society where some were good and others evil. Such a mixture of good and evil leads to constant confusion, where one doesn't know what is good, what is not. But where evil only is esteemed, there is a clear road marked out for us and all, endowed with the same tastes, the same desires, march toward the same end, and are content. However, fools will tell you that evil does not make one happy. This is true only when, as in our present state of things, there is one vast stupidity, which we call custom, or tradition, in exalting the good. But let us esteem evil as though it were an old custom or tradition, and men would reverence it, and follow its many byways. Not merely because it was permitted, for there is always a keen pleasure in doing what is forbidden; but because men would then be free of that fear which hinders the natural pleasure of crime. Let us take, for instance, a society in which incest is considered a crime. Whoever abandons himself to it is unhappy, because laws, opinions, conventions come to freeze up his pleasures. Whoever wishes to abandon himself to it and is afraid is just as unhappy. So you see, the laws which make incest a crime bring nothing but unhappiness. But in a society based on evil, where incest would not be a crime, those who didn't desire it would not be unhappy; those who did would be happy. Therefore, the society which allowed this act would be more suitable to men than the other which didn't. And so it is the same with all the other actions wrongly considered criminal. From this point of view, where these actions are forbidden, a lot of people are made unhappy; but in allowing them nobody can complain, for he who likes whatever action pleases him delivers himself up to it in peace. The others remain in a painless indifference, or are compensated for the wrongs they may receive by a lot of other wrongs which they in their turn are allowed the pleasure of committing. Now you see that in a society built on principles of good nobody is happy; but many are unhappy. So let not those who follow virtue be overweening in worshipping it; the constitution of our societies forces us to it. It is purely an affair of circumstances and convention. Really, that mankind loves it so much is fantastic, but does not make virtue on that account any lovelier!"

This long harangue made it quite evident to Justine that her constant urge to convert would have to be satisfied elsewhere; and so she turned to Rosalie, whom she found more amenable to tender sentiments. She was very eager to convert her to religion. But to succeed in this it was important to get a priest into her confidence. She was confronted with great difficulties, for Rodin, who had a horror of priests and Christianity, would not allow one into his house. And it was just as difficult for Justine to take Rosalie out to a priest, because Rodin never let his daughter leave the house. She could do nothing, therefore, but bide her time and wait for a more auspicious moment to carry out her religious plans. In the meantime she tried to teach her its virtues, and reveal to her the dogmas and mysteries of the church.

"Oh, Rosalie!" said Justine, "can men be so blind not to know there is a future life waiting for him! Is it not enough to be able to know God and worship Him! Does He not set before us His own virtue as an example! Can the Creator of so many wonders be aught but good! And can we please God if we be not good! Should not our gratitude to Him make us love Him! Are not the beautiful things of life and this universe, which we can enjoy, something to be thankful for! Our duties to God are the same as our duties to men, and our devotion to either one brings happiness to the other. Is it not sweet to feel that we make ourselves worthy of God simply by being good and bringing contentment on earth, and that this simple worthiness will bring us near His throne! Ah, Rosalie! how blind are they who wish to rob us of this hope! Duped by their horrible passions, they deny these eternal truths. They say *we* are deceived, not they. By acknowledging these truths they fear the loss of their sinful voluptuousness. But, when their passions grow dim, and the veil is rent asunder, and the imperious voice of God is heard, how bitter must be their remorse! Only in this state, when man's reason is calm, his lust quieted, can he seek the divine and behold the truth. Only at such moments should we believe what he says. During such moments we all reach out for God, this Holy Being Whom we may have formerly disregarded. We implore Him and He consoles us! We pray to Him and He hears us! Ah, Rosalie, why should I deny Him, why should I neglect Him who is so necessary to my happiness? Why should I say with the lost man there is no God? The heart of the reasonable man offers me every moment proofs of this Divine Being's existence! Is it then better to rave with fools than think rightly with wise men? And so if there be a God this God deserves a worship; and the foundation of this worship is virtue!"

With these impassioned words and many others of a like nature, Justine soon made a good Christian out of Rosalie, who was still as yet a novice in these matters. But in the precariousness of her present situation Rosalie found little means of putting these fine principles into practice. Forced to obey her father, she yielded to all his whims; she could do nothing more about it than show a feeling of revulsion and disgust. But even that with a man like Rodin was quite dangerous. This greatly worried Justine. She was in constant fear of the serious harm that might at any time befall her young friend, whom she finally persuaded to make an escape. They made definite plans for this hazardous enterprise and set a time two days ahead to carry it out. But the very next day Rosalie suddenly disappeared. Justine could find out neither where she was nor what had become of her. She questioned Rodin, the two maids, but they sounded vague and said she had gone to spend a few weeks at the house of a distant cousin. Justine then asked Rodin why her departure was so sudden and had been concealed from her. He said he had wished to prevent a painful scene, but that she would soon see her friend again. Justine was not reassured by these evasive replies, and could not bring herself around to believe that Rosalie would leave without saying a word to her; and from what she knew of Rodin, was there not much to fear for the fate of the poor girl. She was resolved at all costs to locate her whereabouts.

Alone in the house the next day, she made a careful search in all its parts. From the bottom of a very dark cellar she thought she heard some moans. She drew quickly near and got close to a narrow door blocked up by a huge pile of wood in the far corner of the cellar. She removed the obstacles in her way and was sure she heard Rosalie.

"Therese! oh, Therese! is it you?" Justine plied her with a barrage of questions that Rosalie had great difficulty answering. But Justine gathered that Doctor Rodin and a colleague of his were going to make Rosalie the subject of a ghastly experiment. She searched for the key to the door on all sides, but soon gave up all hope of finding it. She swore to Rosalie however, that she would come again next day. She begged her not to lose hope, said that she would lodge a complaint before a court of justice, and that she would set her free from the fate before her, cost what it might.

She then went upstairs. Rodin and his colleague,

Rombeau, were having supper together that evening. With only a vague idea of their intentions, she hid near their room to get a fuller knowledge of what they were really up to. When they came in and sat down to table their conversation readily appraised Justine of their plans.

"Never," said Doctor Rodin, "will anatomy be at its last degree of perfection until an examination is made of the arteries of a live young girl. Only in this way can we get a complete analysis."

"Your daughter is just what we want. I'm glad that at last you have made up your mind," said Rombeau.

"Of course I have," Rodin replied. "It is stupid that absurd family considerations should hinder the progress of the sciences. Have great men ever allowed themselves to be subjected to such despicable ties? And when Michelangelo wanted to paint a Christ after nature, did he make it a case of conscience to crucify a young man and copy him in agonies? Why should it not be the same with our art! How much more important in our case: we sacrifice one person to save a million. Should we hesitate at such a price!"

"This is the only way of instructing ourselves," said Rombeau. "In the many hospitals I've worked in during my early years I have watched a thousand similar experiments. But the child being your daughter, I was afraid you might hesitate."

"Why?... because she is my daughter! A fine reason!" said Rodin. "What place do you imagine that has in my heart? One is master to take back what he has bestowed. The right of disposing of one's children has never been disputed among any of the ancient peoples of the earth. The Persians, Medes, Armenians, Greeks fully enjoyed this privilege. The laws of Lycurgus, that model of legislators, not only left to the fathers all rights over their children, but also condemned to death those a parent did not wish to bring up, or were deformed. Many savages kill their children as soon as they are born. Cook found this custom throughout all the South Sea Islands. And didn't Romulus permit infanticide? The laws of the Twelve Tables likewise tolerated it, and up to the time of Constantine the Romans exposed or killed their children with impunity. Aristotle himself advises this supposed crime; the Stoics thought it praiseworthy, and it is still customary among the Chinese. Every day in the streets and canals of Pekin are to be found thousands abandoned or murdered by their parents. And in this wise empire to get rid of a child a father need only place it in the hands of a judge. According to the laws of Parthes people used to kill their sons, daughters or brothers even at a marriageable age; Caesar found this custom among the Gauls. Several passages of the Pentateuch show that it was permitted to kill one's children among God's people: God himself exacted it from Abraham. A celebrated modern author says that it was for a long time thought that the prosperity of empires depended upon the servitude of children. This opinion was based upon the soundest reasoning. Well, a country for, its own whim can sacrifice twenty or thirty thousand subjects in one day, and to think that a father cannot become master of the life of his own children! What an absurdity! How silly and weak they are who are held back by such ties! The authority of the father over his children is the only real authority, and the foundation of all others. Only in our barbarous France a false and ridiculous pity imagines this right should be curbed! No!" Rodin continued, "no, my friend, I shall never understand how a father, who was eager to bestow life, is not free to bestow death! We set too high a value upon this life, which makes us talk nonsense about a man's wanting to get rid of another. We think that existence is the greatest of goods and stupidly imagine we are committing a crime doing away with those who are enjoying it. But the ending of this existence and what follows it is no more an evil than life is a good. If nothing is destroyed, nothing lost in nature, if all the decomposed parts of any body only await the dissolution to reappear immediately under fresh forms, is not murder a trivial matter! How can a man have enough impudence to find any harm in it! Were it but a question of my own beliefs I should find the whole thing very simple: my art is very useful to men and my daughter's destruction is necessary to my art. Serving such a great benefit, it is no longer an evil. It is the best, my friend, the wisest, the most useful of all actions. Only in depriving oneself of it could there be a crime!"

"Oh!" cried Rombeau, filled with enthusiasm over these opinions. "I approve of you, my dear. Your wisdom enchants me! But your indifference astonishes me. I thought you were amorous..."

"I!.... in love with a girl! Ah, Rombeau, I thought you knew me better! I make use of such creatures when I have nothing better. You understand, Rombeau. Chilperic, the most voluptuous of the kings of France, felt the same way about it. He used to say that one could, worse come to worse, make use of a woman, but on the express condition of doing away with her as soon as one had enjoyed her. Now this little plaything has served me for five years; it is high time she paid for having dulled my pleasures!"

They were almost through with their dinner. Justine clearly saw by their manner, talk and the delirium into which they were slowly working themselves, that Rosalie was to be sacrificed that very same evening. Not a moment was to be lost. She immediately flew to the cellar, desperate in her wish to do something to forestall them in what their talk and intentions forboded.

"Oh, Rosalie darling!" she cried, "not a moment to be lost... the monsters.... it is for this evening... they'll soon be here.... I"

And she made a violent effort to break the door. But Rodin and Rombeau, informed by one of the maids, suddenly appeared.

"What are you up to?" cried Rodin, stopping Justine. "Therese, that is the effect then of your mighty principles of virtue.... to rob a father of his daughter!"

"Certainly!" Justine said firmly. "That's just what I should do when this father is barbarous enough to plot against the life of his daughter!"

"Ah, eavesdropper! A servant's most typical vice! We'll take both you and Rosalie upstairs; we must finish this business!"

Justine and Rosalie were dragged upstairs into Rodin's room, where Rosalie was tied to the bedposts. Frantic with rage, the two men turned upon Justine and loaded her with great abuse; they threatened to dissect her alive. They were beating her with their hands. "Let me take her!" cried Rombeau. Justine flung herself at his feet, offered him her life, anything, but begged them only to honor her virtue.

"But since you are no longer a maiden," said Rombeau, "what difference does it make! You will be guilty of nothing. We are only going to do what has already been done to you. Besides, there'll be no sin on your conscience; it is force which takes everything from you!" While bantering her in this manner he was already forcing her toward the sofa.

"No, let's not waste our energies on this slut. Remember, we need it for the proposed operations on Rosalie, which must not be delayed any longer. We can punish this trollop here in some other way." Saying this, he put an iron bar into the fire. "Yes, let's punish her in a worse way. Let's brand her! Let's tattoo her! It will have her hanged or starved!"

And while Rombeau held her rigid Rodin riveted the red iron, with which felons were ordinarily branded, into the back of her shoulder, turning it round and round, and filling the room with an acrid smell and her shriller and shriller cries.

"Let her show herself now!" Rodin muttered.

When Justine came out of a swoon they dressed her and strengthened her with a few drops of whiskey. And under cover of the night's darkness they carried her to the woods and abandoned her there. They convinced her of the danger of making any recrimination, since she was branded as a criminal.

Anybody but Justine would have cared very little about this mark of infamy. It could easily have been proven that this brand was not the mark of an official tribunal. There was really nothing to be afraid of. But her weakness, her innate shyness and timidity, and the terror of her recent misfortunes in Paris and those at the Castle de Bressac, all astounded and frightened her. She had now but one thought, one hope, to get away to some remote place where she might be sheltered from the world's evil and brutality.

Chapter 9

ON THE FOURTH day she reached Lieusaint. This route led to the south, and she decided to follow it. She thought that in this distant region at the end of France she would at last find that peace and happiness which in her own native provinces so persistently fled right from under her grasp.

Justine was not completely discouraged. She thought she might even have been worse off; for whatever may have been her pains and misfortunes, she felt that at least her innocence was left her. Solely the victim of a few ruthless men, she still, nevertheless, considered herself an honest girl; albeit some time ago, in an unfortunate moment when her senses were stunned, she was actually deprived of what she had always been taught to be the highest and proudest claim of that kind of girl; but all traces of that sad deprivation were now gone and she had nothing really with which to reproach herself. At any rate, her heart was still pure. Moreover, she had a little money about her, which she was glad had never been taken from her. She hoped it would carry her over until she found another job. She did not think there would be any difficulty finding work; she was in good health and possessed a lovely figure, which to her grief people praised only too much. Her only handicap seemed to be her virtue; but on the other hand it was her greatest consolation, and she was sure Heaven would eventually reward it. The sentiments of religion never at any time abandoned her. The vain sophisms of free-thinkers she thoroughly despised, and believed them more the outcome of passion than firm conviction. It was only necessary to refute them with her conscience and her heart.

So with much hope and courage in her heart she continued on toward Sens, stopping there just for a few days. In this town she could easily have found work, but having heard much about Dauphiny she proceeded farther in that direction.

One day the first week of August she was leaving Auxerre. It was a blistering hot day, and about two miles out of town she turned into a road that took her to a small hill covered with large shady trees. She was tired and drowsy from the heat, and stretched herself out under the cool shade. She soon fell asleep.

She was suddenly roused from a heavy sleep by a disturbing dream she had, in which her sister, Juliet, her friend, Rosalie, Bressac and Doctor Rodin were all mixed up together. She sat right up, and with half-closed eyes gazed dreamily around at the surrounding country. From her elevated position she had a fine view in front of her: meandering streams losing themselves among wooded hills rolling away as far as the eye could see. Far in the distance away to the right she descried a small belfry rising gracefully into the air.

"What a lovely solitude!" Justine hummed to herself. "Makes me envious. Must be the retreat of some holy, cloistered nuns devoted to God. Maybe some hermits consecrated to religion. Ah, all the virtues must dwell under that sacred roof I How my heart goes out to it.... if I could but lose myself in such a solitude..."

She was lost in her musings when suddenly a shepherd girl passed by. Justine asked what place it was; and was told that it was a Temple of Mota occupied by four anchorites whose piety, chastity and holiness were seldom equalled.

"People go there," said the shepherdess, "once a year on pilgrimage to a miraculous spirit, from whom pious folk obtain everything they wish for."

Justine was strangely touched, and wanted to go at once and beg assistance from this supernatural being. She asked the girl if she would go there and say a prayer with her. The shepherdess found it impossible to go with her, but, pointing the way to her, said it was easy to find; and that the first brother of the temple, the most holy and worthy of men, would receive her well.

"They call him Dom Severino," she continued. "He's an Italian, a descendant of royalty. Go to that strange solitude, miss; you'll come back feeling much better."

Encouraged by these words, she could no longer restrain her eagerness to go and visit this unique temple. She gave the girl a coin for her trouble and immediately set out.

When she got down into the plain the belfry was hidden to view, and she had nothing but a forest way off in the distance to guide her.

It was some time before she even got half way to it. She realized that she had greatly misjudged the distance. But it was still daylight, and she continued on, hoping to reach the temple before night set in.

The country was wild and desolate, with not a house anywhere to be seen.

The sun had already started to set. She was walking rapidly along a small out-of-the-way path hemmed in on both sides by a jungle-like undergrowth, when she heard the sound of a bell. She hastened her steps in its direction, and soon came upon a wide level road with hedges. A little farther on she espied the temple, set in an isolated spot in a wilderness of woods. It lay deep in a hollow, and she had to go a long way down before actually reaching it.

Adjacent to the convent walls stood a gardener's cottage, where visitors applied before entering.

Justine asked the porter if she could speak to the first brother. He asked what she wanted. She said that religious devotion brought her to this pious retreat, that she wanted to be confessed and say a prayer to the great spirit.

The gardener rang and went inside the convent. As it was late and the brothers at supper, he was a long time in returning. At last he came back with one of the hermits.

"Miss," the gardener said, "this is Dom Clement, the procurator of the house, and he comes to see if what you want is worth the trouble of disturbing the first brother."

Dom Clement was a middle-aged man, very big and bulky. There was a savage look in his face that unnerved her.

"What do you want?" he said to her with the sourest look, in a loud voice. "Is this the time to come into a temple! You look like a fly-by-night to me!"

"Good man!" said Justine very faintly, throwing herself at his feet, "I thought it was always time to come to a house of light! I've come a long way, filled with fervor and devotion! I beg to tell you my story, if possible, and when my conscience is known to you, you shall see whether or not I am worthy enough to throw myself at the feet of the great spirit!"

"But this is not the time to talk," the monk said, softening his manner. "Where will you spend the night? We have no night refuge. You should have come in the morning."

The hermit then told her to wait, and went inside to his chief. In a little while Dom Severino, the first brother himself, came out to the gardener's cottage and amiably invited Justine to enter the temple with him.

Dom Severino was a very handsome man. Though strong and vigorous-looking, there was a reassuring softness about him. He was dignified and graceful, and had a natural, attractive courteousness in his general tone. Under the spell of his kind manner Justine recovered from her initial fright.

"My dear girl," he said kindly, "although it is an unreasonable hour, and we are not accustomed to receive so late, I shall, nevertheless, hear your tale. I will advise you later how to pass the night decently. Tomorrow you can kneel to the idol of Mota which brought you here."

They both entered the temple and the doors were closed behind them. A lamp was lit near the six-sided altar. Bidding Justine take her place, the hermit sat down and persuaded her to confess herself to him freely with all confidence.

At ease with a man who appeared so gentle, Justine humbled herself and related all her faults, both real and imaginary, and hid nothing from him. She told him all her misfortunes, with many of their particulars. The hermit listened to her very attentively, and with an expression of compassion and a gesture of solicitude made her repeat certain particularly unsavory episodes. Justine was astonished that he lay such stress on obscene details, but she naively told him everything, nevertheless, in a thoroughly sincere and forthright manner.

"What, all that happened to you?" The hermit then rose, took Justine by the hand and continued, "Well, come, my child, I shall give you the sweet satisfaction of receiving a blessing tomorrow at the feet of the Lord Moto. But let us begin by providing for your first wants." And he led her towards the back of the church.

"What?" said Justine, very uneasy. "What, my father, inside?"

"Where then? charming pilgrim," he said, leading her into the interior. "What, you're afraid to pass the night with four good hermits! Oh, you'll see how well we'll entertain you. If we do not give you much pleasure, you will surely serve ours greatly."

Justine felt faint with terror, and a cold clammy sweat crept slowly over her body.

It was now very dark, with not a single light to lead their way. Her frightened imagination brought before her mind all sorts of scarifying visions, which unnerved her completely and made her knees sag., Compelled to support her from falling the hermit suddenly changed the politeness of his manner and upbraided her severely. "Listen, wench," he said, "you've got to walk! Stop your stalling! it will all be useless!"

They walked blindly on for some time, through a bewildering maze of sharp winding turns. Finally, they arrived at a long staircase. After climbing many steps, they were dazzled by a bright light from an open door. They entered a large hall, magnificently lit up. Three men and four girls were seated round a table. Four other women were serving them.

This spectacle made Justine shiver.

Severino pushed her rudely in. "Gentlemen," he announced, "allow me to introduce to you a rare phenomenon. Here is a pure girl who at the same time carries on her shoulder the brand of a whore! And in her conscience all the frankness, all the simplicity of a maiden! Ah, Clement, what cheer she'll bring to your old soul!"

"Ah, strumpet!" said Clement, rising and going towards her, half-drunk, "the meeting is a pleasant one and I wish to verify the facts!"

When Justine drew back, the first brother said to her curtly,, "Stop these apish tricks. Resistance is useless; you'd better imitate your companions over there. You say that you have experienced many things, but that you are proud you are still almost a virgin. Can one still be a virgin at your age? Don't you think it's about time? Do you see those women there; when they first came here they too put up a resistance. But they changed their minds right quick, just as you will, when they saw what that would bring them." And he pointed out to her various rods, ferrules, switches, ropes and other instruments of torture hanging on the walls. "That is what we use with rebellious girls. And what is more, what do you expect here? Humanity? Being inhuman is one of our pleasures. Religion? It is null in our eyes. You will find here only cruelty, violence and debauchery. It's best for you to submit; it's all you can do. See how inaccessible this place is? Not a stranger ever showed his face here. If the temple were plundered, burned down, this retreat here would still remain undiscovered. It is an insulated pavilion shut in on all sides. And here you are within it, my girl, with four men who certainly haven't a mind to spare you. Your tears and entreaties will but rouse our violence more. To whom then can you turn? You see how it is then, Therese. There is no power can tear you from our hands, or preserve your virtue any longer—not even a miracle. You'll serve our fits and like it, and say no more about it. Now prepare yourself, or we'll soon enough show you what cruel torture you risk disobeying us!"

Notwithstanding the implacable intention of his words, Justine felt that a great guilt would thereafter burden her conscience did she not desperately cling to the last straw which she thought might still preserve her virtue; and she threw herself at Severino's feet and made wet with her tears the quadrumvir's knees. With all the desperate eloquence of a lost soul she besought him not to take advantage of her pitiful condition. She tried to move him with everything she imagined most persuasive, with everything her fancy thought most pathetic. But it was all to no purpose. She always managed to forget that in the eyes of such men tears had an additional attraction; and found it difficult to be convinced that trying to placate them simply salted their dish and whetted their appetites.

"Grab her!" Severino said in a rage. "Grab her, Clement! Let her learn that it's not with us folk pity stifles nature!"

Clement frothed. The resistance Justine put up threw him into a very mettlesome humor. He got hold of her with his long arms and threatened her with all kinds of obscenities.

"What a lovely creature!" said Severino. "May God strike me dead if ever I've seen one better made!"

"Gentlemen!" he continued, "let's put order into our proceedings. You know our formulas of reception. Let her undergo them all—let us omit nothing. And let the other women get ready to assist us in our game and supply the necessary wants."

A ring was immediately formed and Justine placed in the center of it, where for a considerable length of time she was separately badgered by each of the four wayward hermits in turn.

Severino could no longer contain himself, and like an animal ready to devour its victim, "Come!" he said impatiently, "let us each find our due!"

They threw her down... poor little Justine—she fetched awful cries; she never suffered so much in all her life.

Clement then came up with an armful of rods and a strange gleam in his eyes. "It's me who'll take vengeance for you, my brother! It's me who'll correct this beast for resisting you!" he rambled on incoherently. And he twisted Justine about one of his knees. As a prelude he first tried his lashes lightly; but soon fired with mad lust, he struck with all his might. No part of the poor girl escaped his ferocity. And then each of the quadrumvirs took turns again.

When the preliminary ceremonies were at an end, the first brother ordered some of the women to make Justine eat something. But so great was her despair, she was stubborn in her refusal. And little wonder, for she was wont to place all her pride, her happiness, in her virtue; and being a *good* girl had always consoled her for her misfortunes; but now she was too grievously afflicted by its loss; and at the hands of hermits, from whom she anticipated nothing but help and consolation. It was so irreparable a loss to her that she was shaken with violent sobs, and her cries made the vault ring. Rolling on the ground, she dug her nails into her breasts, tore her hair and begged to be done away with altogether.

Such a spectacle fanned the fire of the brothers' exhausted passions.

"Ah!" said Severino, "I never enjoyed a finer scene! My friends, it's extraordinary I She's an extraordinary woman!"

"Let's take her again!" Clement said. "We'll teach her how to howl!"

In a second orgy they wreaked their every whim upon her, until finally the first brother said, "That's enough for the first day. We must now let her see that her women companions are no better treated."

They sat Justine in a high arm chair, and she was forced to watch other scenes, which were about to end the night's orgies.

The hermits got in line and all the other women filed off before them, receiving once more, as a final salute, the lash of their whips.

The ceremonies over, the four hermits ate and drank to retrieve their strength.

At last Justine was placed by the first brother under the care of one of the women, called Omphale, who was charged to instruct and install Justine in her new home.

This first night, fagged and exhausted, Justine heeded nothing. In the room she was placed she vaguely noticed other women who had not been present at the supper table.

Omphale left her alone, and Justine fell heavily into bed.

All through the night she was restless and tossed in her sleep, which made her torpid brain a prey to the nightmarishness of her waking hours.

Chapter 10

THE HIGH Temple of Mota belonged to the cult of Shaam. For more than a hundred years it existed on the same footing, and all the brothers who came to it helped conserve and extend the tradition of this venerable institution so gay and pleasurable to their fancies. The present first brother, Dom Severino, was one of the most prurient men of the Shaamanite Order. He was an Italian and a descendant of royalty, and on very friendly and intimate terms with many in high places. He had himself placed in the temple so that he could spend the declining years of a long life devoted to the interests of the cult in pleasant retirement and good works, and all in all lead what he thought a really appropriate life. It was only since his time that the pretended miracles of the great spirit strengthened the reputation of the convent, and kept people from noticing too closely what went on within. The cult's leader himself, whether apprised or not of what was going on inside the temple, gave little attention to it and never put in an appearance. Indeed very few people came to it, except toward the festival time, which was that of the Feast of Light. And when they did come the first brother took care to receive them kindly. Through an appearance of holiness and austerity visitors were easily imposed upon. They went away extremely pleased, with nothing but praise for the quadrumvirs.

The temple was supported by huge funds. The four hermits living in it were at the head of the Shaamanite Order, and were very rich in their own rights. Independent of the immense funds contributed by the Order of Shaamanites for the keeping of this retreat, to where in his turn each member of the Order nourished the hope of eventually passing on, those living in the temple donated a large portion of their own wealth to its upkeep. More than a hundred thousand dollars a year was used for the expenses of the house and for kidnapping fresh recruits.

The hermits employed twelve confidential women to bring them a regular supply of new girls, who had to be of aristocratic birth. The brothers were extremely fastidious in their choice of material. Mostly all their women were gathered together from the rank and file of the nobility. Omphale was the daughter of a famous count and, carried away in Paris at the age of twelve, she was destined one day to come into a dowry of several hundred thousand francs. She was stolen from the arms of her governess, who was taking the child out for a ride into the country. The governess later disappeared; she was most likely brought over. So with the other women: their fathers were for the most part dukes, counts, barons and marquises.

In capturing women great precautions were taken and seldom were there any complaints.

With every new arrival at the pavilion one of the old stock was gotten rid of. This practice was called *reforming* a girl. It was a strange custom, and a perplexing mystery to the girls, who could not say what became of them after being *reformed.* But they had strong suspicions that they were brutally done away with and their departure from the temple led only to some sinister end; for like Gilles de Rais, the famous Bluebeard, these monks found an exalted enjoyment in murder and mutilation. They were in the habit of enjoying only through suffering, revelling in tortures and torments; and in murder they sought some way of reaching the complete and perfect expression of the mad delirium of their senses. Every girl that left the pavilion promised the others to make a complaint when she got out; but never were they heard from again. This terrible uncertainty was tormenting. Omphale herself had seen more than two hundred girls *reformed;* what became of them all? she wondered. The hermits were queer about *reforming* a girl. They had no regular rule; it was just a whim with them: one day they got rid of a girl only enjoyed the day before, and on the other hand held on to a woman with whom for the past ten years they had glutted themselves. One never knew who was going next.

Though the girls kept going and coming and there were always new faces among them, the same hermits remained in the temple a long time. Dom Antonin had been there ten years; Clement, eighteen; Jerome, thirty; Dom Severino, the first brother, twenty-five.

It was almost impossible for any of the girls to escape; had it been feasible, they would often have attempted it. The pavilion was laid out like a fortress. Behind the temple proper, in back of the altar, a door concealed in the wainscotting and opened by a hidden spring led to a long and dark trench, through which on the first night of her arrival Justine was taken from the temple to the secret pavilion. This trench passed under a deep moat. On the other side it rose again to a level about six feet underground and ran along in zigzagging curves some distance until it reached the subterranean parts of the pavilion.

The pavilion was a very low structure, and was completely lost to view among rows of high, thick, bushy hedges that ran round all its sides. The roof of the pavilion was very thick and surmounted on the outside by a cistern full of clay in which evergreen shrubs matching the surrounding hedges were planted, giving one the complete illusion of a single dense thicket.

There was but one story above the ground, which contained the two main seraglios, but underground there were three more floors.

This inaccessible retreat gave the hermits complete assurance, which greatly stimulated their ferocity.

Every morning at nine all the hermits went back to the temple. But they left one man behind, whom they styled the *Guard-Regent*. He remained all day in the pavilion. They returned at five in the evening with the necessary supplies, which were given to the cook, and the rest of the night they spent in the pavilion.

The women followed a daily routine. Although the hermits' supper kept them up very late, they had to be up punctually at nine every morning. About this time the *Day-Regent* came to pay them his usual morning visit. He seldom left without a scene of voluptuousness in which all the girls were commonly employed. The first ceremonies over, breakfast was served. Until evening the girls had nothing more to do. But at seven some of them were called to supper with the hermits, and were generally detained until far into the night.

The first of every month each brother adopted a girl to serve him for that period in the duties of private chambermaid and general handy-woman. She was called the *guard-girl*. She had many mean services to perform. Every evening the moment it struck five the *guard-girl* left the dormitory and went down to the hermit she served. She never left his side until he was ready to leave for the temple the next morning. But upon his return she had to take him up again. She was forced to put up with all his whims, cuffs, floggings and various enjoyments, and the slightest repugnance to any of the odious services to be performed was punished by severe tortures. She accompanied him everywhere, dressed and undressed him, waited on him hand and foot. She was always wrong, always beaten; and at the supper table her place was behind her master's chair, or at his feet, or under the table like a dog, or on her knees.

The whip was an important stimulant to the hermits' lubricities, and combining pleasure with correction they disciplined the girls mostly by lashing them. The faults committed were of many kinds, each one having its own particular punishment. Thirty lashes were inflicted for anyone not up at the prescribed hour in the morning. For negligence or refusal in cooperating with the orgies, two hundred lashes were given. This last regulation often caught the girls falling short through no fault of their own. But the correction had to be undergone, nevertheless; complaints or alibis were never listened to. For misbehavior in the dormitory: sixty lashes. For tokens of tears, sorrow or remorse, or religious devoutness: two hundred lashes. For the merest look of repugnance to any of the hermits' propositions: two hundred lashes. The discovery of cabals or evil counsels: three hundred lashes. For schemes of suicide or refusals to take proper nourishment: two hundred lashes. To be wanting in proper respect toward the hermits: three hundred lashes. And for undertaking to escape or revolt: nine days in the dungeon and three hundred lashes daily.

It was a very long list and was posted up in conspicuous places inside the pavilion.

Chapter 11

HER FIRST morning in the temple, when Justine awoke, she found herself in a large dormitory with eight small, clean beds ranged along the wall. To the right of each bed there was a small private room with one window, barred with iron gratings inside and out, high above the ground. There were seven other girls living in the same room.

She felt more dead than alive and was prepared for worse things to come. But a prayer greatly fortified her spirit.

At nine o'clock Dom Antonin appeared and the girls were called together and according to custom formed in line. He threw a cursory glance over them all and having counted them sat down. Looking at Justine, he asked her how she was feeling. Justine returned his look with tears in her eyes. "You'll get used to it," said the hermit, laughing. "There isn't a house in France where girls are better trained." He gave the girls a long lecture on the duties of women, and then addressed himself to Justine again, which made her shudder. Every gesture, every movement, which referred her to these men was like a sentence of death. He told her she was to appear toward evening at Dom Clement's private cell and act as his *guard-girl,* that Dom Clement would give her all necessary instructions. After he left breakfast was served.

That same evening when Clement came into his private cell Justine was already there. She fell to her knees and pleaded with him for mercy, but sternly he told her to rise. "Therese," he said, "you are going to suffer!" And his eyes forboded it. For fear of irritating him still further she remained silent, sucking in her breath in such terror that sweat covered her forehead and tears made her eyes burn. He wheeled her around and proceeded to scourge her with long slender rods that bit fiercely into her flesh. "You please me," he said. "I have never whipped anybody who has given me so much pleasure!"

Exhausted at last, Clement said, "Let us lie down; perhaps it's too much for you, Therese. Not for me, though—I can never have enough. One doesn't get tired of this sport so easily; it's really such good fun. Ah, dear girl, what joy the sufferings of others bring us. Increasing these delights, that's our stumbling block, however. But where there's a will there's a way!"

When he seemed appeased Justine timidly reproached him for his insanities.

"The most ridiculous thing in the world," Clement said to her, "is to want to dispute one's tastes. How silly to blame or punish or stop them, if they don't happen to conform to our own ideas about things! My dear Therese, what men will never understand is that there are no kind of tastes, however odd or criminal, but depends on our nature; we are born that way. It's in us, and what right, I ask, has anybody to want us to change them to something unnatural. The laws are made for man's happiness, are they not? What right then have they to punish a man who cannot correct himself, or could only correct himself at the expense of his happiness? But even then, can one change his tastes? Is it in his power to undo himself, his very nature? Can one become something not in him? Can you ask a man with a long nose to have a small one? Now try and understand, Therese—you're not altogether a stupid girl—try and understand what I'm trying to say. You notice you have been the victim of two pronounced tastes we have: first, you are surprised at the filth we wallow in; and second, wonder how we can get such keen voluptuous pleasures out of ferocity and somebody else's suffering. Let us analyze it all, you'll see how simple it is. You say that only nasty and horrible things give us pleasure. But it's only your own imagination thinks them nasty and horrible; ours may be different, and that's what counts. For we get our ideas of things chiefly through the imagination. It's a faculty of the mind which modifies and colors what we see and what we hear and what we smell. And from this we get our thoughts. You don't doubt this imagination is different in every man. That's why we all look at things differently. Therefore, if there exist in the world people whose tastes are opposed to common prejudices, we must neither find fault with nor punish them. We should even give them every means of satisfying themselves without risk; because it no more depended upon them to have this strange taste than it depended upon others to be stupid or witty, or well-shaped or hunchbacked. One's tastes, one's character and temperament is given to him in his mother's womb and nothing later can change it, education nor anything else. A good man or a villain was born such; they simply have acted according to the mental organization given them by nature. Yes, Therese, how strange it is people can understand a difference of taste when it is merely a question of other matters! But when it concerns our pleasures behold what a fuss they make! It's the women, mostly their fault. They are always fretting about their rights; always petty, selfish, they want to lose nothing for themselves, want nothing to be taken away from them. And if anybody finds pleasure in what they can't partake of, behold crimes deserving the gallows! What an injustice, though! Is there only one way of enjoying one's pleasures? Should a man be inventive in the other functions of life and not in his pleasures! As I said before, the man with strange tastes is a sick man, and it is as silly and cruel to punish such a man, whatever his errings, as punish a man, or mock or ridicule him, who is lame. Wouldn't he be normal if he had it in him—who wouldn't! When anatomy is really perfected, it will be clearly shown that all morality is essentially physical. What then will become of your laws, ethics, religion, gibbets, paradise, God and hell, when it is shown that a particular organization of nerves, a peculiar chemical reaction in the body, a certain degree of sourness in the blood makes a man what he is, for better or worse?—Now don't interrupt me/Therese, let me go on with what I want to say. Our cruelty also amazes you. Why? What is the object of the man who enjoys: is it not to give his sense all the stimulus it is susceptible to, so that he may arrive at his last paroxysm better and quicker? The paroxysm, that is the thing! And it is more or less good according to the greater or less activity it finds itself in. To improve it, it is not necessary that it be shared by the woman. Is it not in fact evident that everything the woman shares with us she takes away from us? Why should a woman enjoy while we're enjoying! Is it not a more pleasing sensation to make the woman stop enjoying so that we may enjoy alone and nothing hinder us from being occupied with solely our own enjoyment? Doesn't this really flatter our pride better? Not delicate, I admit. But where does delicacy come in; it's really obnoxious to enjoyment. Delicacy may go hand in hand with love or romance; but loving and enjoying, are entirely two different things. Everyday people love without enjoying and enjoy without loving. Whatever is associated with delicacy goes to the woman's advantage at the expense of the man's. That's just what it should not be; on the contrary it is most essential that man should enjoy at the woman's expense, taking all for himself regardless of the woman. For if selfishness is the first law of nature, how much more so in the pleasures of the passions! With a woman, a man's own delight is all that should concern him. Outside of that there is no relation at all between them; she is merely an abstraction, there to serve him. And if it happens, Therese, that the man is so unfortunately organized that the woman can further subserve his pleasure by suffering, you must admit that he ought to abandon himself to it without remorse, since he is there merely to enjoy himself, nothing else. These are sound principles, Therese. If they're not understood, that's because the world is full of wooden statues, who come, go, eat, digest and act, without rendering an account to themselves of anything. But I can't see why it should be difficult for anybody to understand that selfish enjoyments have more charm than any others. Now that leads up to the whole explanation of what I wish to make you understand.—The emotion of voluptuousness is mostly imagination, the imagination laboring under some obsession. This obsession may be some kind of beauty which stirs it most, or receiving from some object the greatest possible sensation. Now there is no sensation in an object more quickening than suffering; the impressions are positive and do not deceive like those of pleasure, everlastingly simulated by women, but hardly ever felt by them. Besides, what self-love, youth, strength and health are necessary to be sure of giving a woman this doubtful and only slightly satisfactory impression of pleasure! That of pain, though, does not require the least thing or effort; the more defects a man has, the older he is, the less amiable, the better will he succeed. And the end will be more surely reached; since I maintain that one never fires his imagination better than by giving it the strongest possible impression, no matter what way. See how simple it all is, Therese: the only important thing in sensual pleasures is reaching the fullest measure of enjoyment; enjoyment increases in proportion to the intensity or sensation the imagination receives; and the most intense sensation or impression is produced by pain. The voluptuary, therefore, will impose the greatest amount of pain."

"These are terrible systems, Sir!" said Justine. "They lead to cruel things, to sinful tastes!"

"What difference does that make!" replied Clement. "Didn't I just say that we are not master of our tastes I Shouldn't we follow the promptings of our nature? Aren't these tastes also part of nature; we wouldn't have them if they weren't. What do we care what the consequences of these passions are! When one wishes to delight himself by any action, is there any question of consequences!"

"I am not speaking of consequences," Justine interrupted him. "The question is about the thing itself. Surely if you are not stronger than your nature and like to enjoy according to your principles, will you not take to killing?"

"So be it! By tastes bestowed by nature for her own use, who works out her creations through destructions, I shall carry out her own designs. Oh, Therese, is that a crime, to serve nature? And has man the power of committing crimes? And when, preferring his own happiness to that of others, he overthrows and destroys all he finds in his way, has he done anything but serve nature, whose first and surest inspirations prompt him to make himself happy, no matter at whose expense? The system of love for one's neighbor is a fantastic illusion we owe to Christianity, not to nature. Most followers of early religions were weak, plagued and oppressed; of course *they* needed toleration very badly, and were forced by their very weakness to cry out for humanity. It meant their salvation to establish this fabulous relation of one being to another, and their preservation depended upon its success. But the philosopher doesn't admit these relationships. Considering but himself alone, only to himself does he account for everything; and prevails by his own strength. He has recourse to those fine systems of humanity and beneficence only at times for policy's sake."

"Such a man is a monster!" Justine said.

"Such a man is a man of nature."

"He is a ferocious beast!" she retorted.

"Well, if you'll have it so. The tiger, the leopard, like him are created by nature to carry out its intentions. The wolf that devours the lamb and the evil-doer who destroys the object of his passion accomplish the views of their common mother, nature."

"I refuse to admit it!" said Justine.

"That's because you're afraid of being the lamb. Pure selfishness, Therese. If you were the wolf, you'd understand it. Ask the lamb, it will neither understand that the wolf should devour it. But ask the wolf what is the good of the lamb. 'To feed me,' he'll answer. Wolves eating lambs; the weak, victim of the strong—that is nature. Those are her views, her designs: perpetual action and reaction, a host of vices and virtues. In short, a perfect equilibrium essential for the maintenance of the planets and life, without which all would be instantly destroyed. Oh, Therese, this nature would be dismayed if she could reason aloud with us a moment and we told her that those crimes serving her, those forfeits which she requires and inspires us with, were punished by laws. 'Dunce!' she would say, 'eat, sleep, drink, and commit such crimes as seem good to you. They please me and I inspire you with them. Restrain only what irritates me. Learn that you have nothing in you but what belongs to me, nothing but what I have placed there for reasons it does not befit you to know. The most abominable of your actions is, as the most virtuous of others, simply one of the ways of serving me. Therefore do not hold yourself back, and scorn your laws, your social conventions and Gods. Listen to me alone, and know that crime exists only in opposing me!'"

"Oh, good heavens!" cried Justine, "you make me shudder! If there were no crimes against nature, where then does that repugnance we feel for certain actions come from?"

"This repugnance does not come from nature, Therese. It comes from want of habit. Is it not the same with certain foods? We dislike them simply from want of habit in eating them. Are they no good then because we have not cultivated our tastes for them? Let us overcome our habitual tastes and we shall soon agree about the pleasant savor of some of these dishes. This momentary repugnance you just spoke of is really more a craftiness, a coquetry of nature than a warning that the thing outrages her. That is how she prepares us for the pleasures of triumph; she increases thereby those of the action itself. The more an action thwarts our customs and morals, the more it clashes with our social conventions, the more it hurts what we believe to be the laws of nature, so much the more on the contrary is it useful to this same nature. Only through crimes does she enter into her own rights, those rights taken away from her by virtue. If the crime is only slight, it will establish more slowly the equilibrium requisite for her. Let him who thinks of crime, therefore, have no qualms; the greater the crime, the more will he have served nature."

As Justine continued to listen to Dom Clement's systems, her former suspicions of what happened to the girls when taken away from the pavilion came crowding back into her mind; and wanting to feel him out, she ventured several discreet questions.

"At least," she said, "you don't hold forever the victims of your passions. You send them away, no doubt, when you tire of them?"

"Of course you'll go out of here when we four quadrumvirs agree to it. Eventually you'll go."

"But aren't you afraid," asked Justine, "that one of the girls will squeal when out of here?"

"That's impossible!"

"Impossible?"

"Absolutely!" said Clement.

"But why?... Could you explain to me why?"

"No, that is our secret. It'll be impossible, that's all I can tell you," he said. "But you make me talk too much, Therese, I don't know why. I'm tired, now, leave me alone," he added, falling slowly asleep.

Justine no longer doubted that violent measures were taken against the girls *reformed,* and that freedom from the pavilion only meant death.

In a few hours Clement woke up in great agitation and seized her with such force that she thought he was going to choke her. His breathing was quick and his eyes rolled. Muttering nonsense, he demanded she fetch him the rods, with which he started to whip her with renewed energy.

The rest of the night all was quiet. Next morning Clement was gone to the idolatrous temple and Justine went back to the pavilion.

Two nights later Justine guarded Jerome, with whom she suffered the same whims and crotchets experienced in Clement's cell. By the end of a week she went through all the rounds.

Chapter 12

IT WAS near festival time, when many of the old girls were *reformed* and the hermits got new recruits, either by abducting them from within the temple, or having them kidnapped outside. Many of the girls looked to this week with much anxiety, and in the greater part of their conversation they spoke of nothing else. Who was next to go? they wondered among themselves.

At last the famous festival arrived. In order to have the reputation of the temple bruited abroad through the neighboring countryside, the hermits arranged for a miracle. They had Florette, the youngest of the girls, disguised as a handmaiden of Mota, and bound her with invisible cords to a niche in the wall. They told her she was suddenly to raise her arms with compunction to Heaven just as they bowed to the idol. And she was threatened with the most brutal punishment did she utter a word or the miracle failed.

But Florette got through admirably well and the fraud was a great success. The people cried, "Miracle!" left rich offerings to Mota and departed more than ever convinced of the reality of the "Lord of Lords and Lord of All."

To lend a keener edge to the orgies, Florette was made to appear toward night in the same robes of the handmaiden which had won so much homage.

The costume greatly excited the hermits, and they subjected Florette, dressed up as she was, to all their wildest whims. "It's really too bad that this poor girl has to suffer so for the failings of the spirit," the first brother said, in one of his quieter moods.

Then they stretched her flat on a large table. They lit wax candles. They took a token of the great spirit and placing it near her loins, desecrated upon her the most solemn of mysteries.

Unable to bear such a sight, Justine fainted. When she was seen in this state Severino said she was next to serve as altar, in order to make herself more familiar with this ceremony.

They put her in Florette's place, and she was made to

absorb within her the unholy token. The sacrifice was then consummated, and, blaspheming, Severino defiled both Justine and the idolatrous symbol at one and the same time.

She was taken motionless out of their hands. She was in great mental anguish for a long time after. Virtue was a tender sentiment with her, and anything that offended or outraged it made the blood of her heart spurt up.

Next morning Severino entered the girls' room and observing Omphale told her the convent *reformed* her. "The society is fed up on you. Be ready tonight. I'll come for you myself," he said.

Omphale threw herself into Justine's arms and wept.

"What's to become of me?"

"Calm yourself," said Justine, "don't be afraid; everything will be all right."

Nothing happened that day; but about five o'clock the first brother came up for Omphale.

"You ready?"

"Yes, my master," she wept. "I want to say good-bye to my friends."

"Come on, that's not necessary. We haven't time for weeping scenes, they're waiting for us. Come on, hurry!"

Justine asked Severino if she could escort Omphale to the door, but he fixed her with a look that made her recoil. With wistful glances and tears Omphale at last left the pavilion. Justine threw herself down upon her bed and buried her head in despair. But the rest of the girls were resigned by now, and even indifferent.

In less than an hour the first brother came back for those who were to appear at the supper party that night. Justine was one of them.

At the supper party everything went off as before, except that the hermits often whispered together and drank more than usual. But the girls were sent away much earlier and all were allowed to go to bed. In great perplexity, Justine knew not what to conjecture from these circumstances, different as they were from the usual routine. But she was very alert to everything that transpired, and was somehow reassured by a vague and persistent hope that Omphale was safe outside and would help in bringing about her release and liberty.

Three days passed, however, and nothing was heard from Omphale. On the fourth day Justine was again one of the supper party. That night the finest women assisted at the evening rites, and the *guard-girls* were also there.

As they entered they noticed a new arrival.

"Ladies, our new little friend here is going to take Omphale's place!" said the first brother.

She was a fine-looking young creature about sixteen, with a small waist and the loveliest hair and white skin. She was called Octavie. She was carried away by force from her carriage, along with two governesses and three lackeys. Blindfolded, she alone was conveyed to the pavilion at night, and had no knowledge of her whereabouts.

Nobody had as yet spoken a word to her. She raised her tearful eyes shyly to the other girls. For a moment the four hermits gazed admiringly at the girl's beauty, anticipating a great relish.

"Come, fair child," the first brother said with light mockery, pulling her towards him, "come, let us see if the rest of you is as lovely as your face."

Confused and blushing, she tried to squirm out of the hermit's grip and back away; but he shot his arm around her body and tightened his hold. "Understand, little Agnes," he said to her, "understand that that is not the way to behave with your master."

She tried to defend herself, but the ring was already formed around her, which she tried to run through in every direction.

In his last throes, Severino got madly hold of her. She cried bitterly, but was ignored. Between the hermit and the girl there was an enormous inequality, which made Octavie cry again and again for quarter; but slowly, painfully, the gorge of his passion rose, until at last he expired, amid her wild and vain struggles.

"Never was laurel harder!" faltered Severino. "What a creature, a Ganymede of the Gods!"

"I must restore her!" said Antonin, not letting her get up. Fresh cries were heard. "Mota be praised!" he said, "I should have doubted my success without her groans, but my triumph is assured with tears and blood!"

"Indeed!" said Clement, closing up with rods in his hands, "I shall not disturb this sweet attitude either, it is too favorable!"

Jerome's *guard-girl* was now holding Octavie. "Oh, my friends!" he said, exalted, "why not flog the novice who shows so much beauty!"

The rods whizzed through the air and fell with a singing sound upon the girl's flesh. Her cries were submerged beneath a torrent of blasphemies.

Late at night Octavie was sent back to the pavilion. Justine had hoped to comfort her this first night, but she was obliged to guard Severino, whom she seemed to please more keenly than any of the rest of the girls. He longed for her almost every night and constantly sought newer and great refinements, until she thought she was ready to give up the ghost. It seemed to her that she was more in need of consolation than even Octavie.

Chapter 13

JUSTINE HAD long made up her mind to attempt an escape, for which she had made careful preparations almost two months. Without drawing any suspicion, she had already succeeded in sawing through the gratings of the window in her small private room; and there was large enough a hole for her head to pass through. She used an old chisel that she found while serving as *guard-girl* in Dom Clement's cell. And she had enough linen to piece together a long rope. All that was lacking was the ripe moment to execute her plan.

One morning Antonin surprised the girls by making an appearance in their room and announcing that the great Dom Severino, a protege of the Mota himself, had just been appointed First Server of the Shaamanite Order by the rulers of the cult.

The next day Dom Severino set out without seeing the girls, among whom a rumor was soon spread that another first brother; one with even a more notorious reputation for severity, was coming in his place.

He was a great master of discipline, this new brother, and in a long proclamation he had already sent word ahead that the temple was falling short of its old, venerable traditions, and as a result was reaching a critical stage in its long history; that to confront the possibilities of utter extinction severe measures had to be taken. And in this long official document which was executed with an imposing array of seals and ribbons, he laid out an exuberance of regulations to be enforced during his tenure of office. "What is an institution, a nation, a people!" said the document, "without its august traditions, the backbone, prop and support of its very existence!"

This turn of events brought to a head Justine's plan to escape. She felt there was nothing to fear, for even did she fail to make a successful getaway there was nothing to lose; death was her ultimate end one way or the other. But in success there was at least a chance of saving herself.

She chose a time when the hermits had decided to *reform* another of the girls as most propitious for making her escape. The hermits were preoccupied with *reforming* and paid little attention to her. All the girls of the pavilion were at the supper party and Justine was left behind with just another companion, who soon went to bed. It was only the beginning of spring and the nights were still long, greatly favoring her steps. She went quietly into her small room and carefully cleared the breach in the window, which she took pains to cover carefully up every day. Fastening her rope to one of the undamaged bars, she crawled out and slid down to the ground below. Her hands bruised and bleeding, she cut her way through a dense brushwood with Dom Clement's chisel, which she had enough presence of mind not to leave behind. She at last arrived at the brink of a ditch, which was deep, but dry, being in a state of repairs. On the other side, there before her, was the temple and the gardener's cottage adjacent to it outlined in deep shadow. She thought it best not to cross the ditch on this side, and so crawled around to its opposite side, which faced a road leading into the woods. The ditch was lined with rough brick, and she clambered down into it without slipping and got to the other bank, which she had little difficulty climbing, for the wall of the ditch was crumbling with age and had so many holes that it was more like a ladder. When Justine got to the top she ran madly up the road. Before long she was safely out of the woods. She made her way slowly to Dijon, where she thought her complaints would be lawfully received.

Chapter 14

DESPITE THE THORNS which continually beset Justine in her difficult career of virtue, she was always brought back to God and feelings of love and resignation. She was sure that only the intercession of this good God whom she adored made possible her miraculous escape from the High Temple of Mota. And she felt, come what may, He would always sustain her. Were there not others more to be pitied than herself? Yes, deep was her gratitude for His works.

It was with such feelings that Justine rested at an inn lying close by the town of Dijon.

Toward evening, a very short distance from Dijon, two men came quietly up from behind, threw a cloak over her head to prevent her seeing anything or crying out, handcuffed her like a criminal, and dragged her off without saying a word.

They marched with her about two hours along a route that was hidden to her blindfolded eyes. She was breathing with some difficulty and one of the two men proposed giving her more air. They uncovered her head. She thought she was being retaken by agents of the hermits, and was fear-stricken.

"Oh," she said, "where are we going? What are you going to do with me?"

"Calm yourself," one of the men replied, "nothing is going to happen to you. Don't let these precautions we're taking worry you. We are bringing you to a good master. He's got to have a chambermaid for his wife and there's a reason for all this mystery, but you'll be all right."

"Alas, gentlemen, if it's for my own happiness, you don't have to force me. Why be afraid of my running away? I'm a poor orphan, greatly to be pitied; all I ask is a place!"

"She's right!" said one of the men. "Let's put her more at ease and merely hold her hands."

They did so and continued on. Seeing that she was meek and calm, they even spoke to her kindly. At last she learned from them that the man they were taking her to was the Marquis de Gernande, a rich nobleman living alone in the country.

"Alone?"

"Yes, he's a solitary man, a philosopher. He hardly sees anybody."

"But why all these precautions?" Justine asked.

"The reason is, you see our master's wife is a little loose

in her head. She never goes out of her room and must be watched at all times. Now, of course, nobody wants a job like that. If we told you that before you'd never take the job yourself, so we had to take you by force."

"What!" cried Justine. "I shall be a captive near such a woman!"

"Sure, what of it! That's all right, you'll be well taken care of—don't worry about that."

"Oh heavens!"

"Come, come; it's not forever. It's a cinch and there's money in it."

A large house now loomed up in front of them. It seemed empty and deserted as they came up close to it.

Justine was taken to the Marquis; who was stretched out on a low divan. Near him were two young boys dressed very effeminately, their hair done up with much daintiness. They had pretty faces, but so pale that it seemed they were ill.

"Here at last is a girl for you!" said one of the men to the Marquis, motioning to Justine. "She's looking for work. I think she'll do."

"All right, Louis," he replied. "Shut the doors after you and see that nobody comes in until I ring."

The Marquis de Gernande then rose and proceeded to examine Justine's arms. After a rapid and blunt examination he asked her what sort of work she had done before. When Justine told him something of her life he said, "Fine, so much the better; you will only be more useful in my own house. It's really a good thing that hard luck dogs the steps of such abject people crawling near us on the same soil."

"But, sir," said Justine, "I've told you my birth, it is not abject."

"Yes, yes," he brushed her aside, "I'm aware of all that. People always like to pass themselves off as somebody when they are really nobody at all. Mere illusions of pride.

86

Anyway, it's all the same to me: I find you looking like a servant, and dressed like one; and so I'll take you on that footing. Yet," he looked at her sternly, "it all depends on yourself to be happy here. A little patience and discretion, and in a few years I'll discharge you from here with enough money to live comfortably on your own account."

Then he took up her arms again, first one, then the other, which, tucking up her sleeves, he scrutinized very curiously.

"Have you ever been bled before?" he asked. "No, sir," said Justine, surprised at his question. "I must know how you are formed," he said, staring at her crossly. "There must be no defect for the place you have to fill, so show all you bear."

She tried to stop him, but he got angry and told her not to play the prude with him, as he had sure means of getting the upper hand of women. "What you told me about yourself," he said, "doesn't forbode a very lofty virtue. Your resistances are as much out of place as ridiculous!"

She realized she was defenseless with a man who could have reduced her to powder with one blow of his fist, so she submitted.

The Marquis beckoned to his two young attendants, who directly approached Justine and held her, while he, a contrary enthusiast, roughly handled her.

He then pulled her into a neighboring room where two other pretty young men were working at tapestry. They rose when the Marquis entered.

"Narcisse," he said to one of them, "this is my wife's new chambermaid; I must try her out. Hand me the lancets."

Narcisse opened a box and brought out forthwith several instruments for bleeding.

"Place her, Zephire," the Marquis said to the other young man.

She was propped upon her knees at the side of a stool laid

in the center of the room. Her arms were sustained by two black ribbons attached to the ceiling. Lancet in hand, the Marquis approached her. His eyes moist, he was breathless. He tied both her arms, and with quick bird-like movements, he started pricking them. The blood began to spurt, at the sight of which he grunted with pleasure. He went and sat down opposite Justine, about six feet away. The light gown which covered him was soon spread out. Never for a moment did he take his burning eyes from the blood that dripped from her, falling into two white bowls placed under her arms. Zephire and Narcisse clung close down to their master, and he intently watched the red streams pattering into the pans.

Justine felt herself growing terribly weak. "Stop, heavens stop!... have pity..... I'm fainting...." she barely gasped, and she started to sway, but the ribbons kept her from falling. Her head fell to one side on her shoulder and her face was smeared with blood.

On recovering her senses Justine found herself lying in a warm, comfortable bed. Two old women were near her, who brought her some broth as soon as her eyes were opened.

On the morning of the fourth day she was ordered by the Marquis to get up and come and speak with him. She was led into his drawing room, still somewhat weak. "Therese," he said to her, making her sit down, "I'll seldom experiment like that on you again. You'll be useful for other purposes. I just wanted to give you an idea of my tastes. That's how you'll end, though, if you ever betray me in any way, or let my wife get into your graces. But don't imagine I treat her this way because of any hatred or contempt for her. It's just passion. Nothing is like the pleasure I feel in shedding her blood! It simply goes to my head when I see it flowing. I have never enjoyed her in any other way, though it's three years since I married her. Every fourth day she gets the same treatment you experienced. She is hardly twenty, and her youth and the care she gets are what sustain her. Now, you see why I can't let her out or have her see anybody. I pass her off as mad, and her mother, the only relation she has left, living in her castle six miles from here, is so convinced of it that she dares not even come to see her. My wife will go on this way as long as she can, but she'll want for nothing while she lives. As I like to waste her away slowly I'll try to keep her alive as long as possible. When she can no longer hold out, God speed her! She's my fourth woman—pretty soon there'll be a fifth. Nothing troubles me less than a woman's lot. There are so many of them in the world, and it's so sweet to change them! Be this as it may, Therese, your job is to look after her. She loses a regular quantity of blood every four days. She doesn't swoon any more now, she's used to it already. Her faint-ness lasts about twenty-four hours; the other three days she's all right. But you can easily understand that she doesn't like this life very much. She'd do anything to be free, or to let her mother know her true condition. She's already ingratiated herself with two of her maids, but I found them out in time to stop their maneuvers. She has caused the death of those two poor women and regrets it to this day. She is more resigned now and accepts her lot, and promises not to try to win over any more of the chambermaids I bring to her. That is why I am obliged to take maids by force, just as you've been, to avoid lawsuits. Not having taken you at anybody's house, not having to give any account of you to anybody, I can do what I please with you in case you try to betray me. I would get into no trouble even if I killed you. So, my child, you'd better watch your step, I warn you. Any underhandedness and you're as good as dead!"

There was nothing more to be said about it and Justine followed her master. They passed through a long, dark hall. A door was opened and they entered an antechamber, where the same two old women who waited on Justine during her illness rose and introduced them into a large and beautiful apartment. The Marquise, seated on a high chair, embroidering, stood up when she beheld her husband.

"Sit down," the Marquis said to her. "I'll allow you to listen to me seated. At last I've found a maid for you. I hope you'll remember what happened to the other two and won't get this girl into the same trouble."

"It would be useless," said Justine, eager to help the unfortunate woman and trying to cloak her real intentions before the Marquis. "Yes, madame, I might as well tell you to your face that it would be useless. I'll tell anything you say to me to the Marquis. I'm not going to risk my life for you."

"I'll do nothing to compromise you," the Marquise replied, not sensing Justine's true motives. "Don't be uneasy, I will want you to do nothing outside of the line of your duty."

"That'll be wholly yours, madame, but nothing further!"

Delighted, the Marquis shook Justine's hand and whispered in her ear, "Good, Therese! your fortune is made if you do as you say."

He then showed her to her room, which was adjacent to that of the Marquise. He made her observe that the entire apartment was shut in by strong doors, and all openings secured by double gratings, which left little hope of escape.

"There is the terrace," he added, leading her into a small garden which was on a level with the apartment. "I don't think you'll be foolish enough to try to scale its walls. My wife may come here and breathe the fresh air as much as she likes, but you will keep her company. That's about all for the present—good-bye."

Justine went in to see her new mistress. They looked each other over without speaking. Madame de Gernande was a young woman not yet twenty. She was tall, slender and graceful. She was fair but had dark, beautiful eyes full of tender expression. Small nose, white skin, a well moulded chin, a small mouth with gleaming teeth, a fine oval contour to her face,—the Marquise was a woman of beauty. And although slender, she was well and firmly built. She seemed, moreover, good-natured and sensible. "On what day were you bled last, madame?" Justine asked her.

"Three days ago. Tomorrow again,—yes, tomorrow you'll see this fine scene!"

"Doesn't it weaken you?" Justine asked.

"Weaken me! Good heavens! I'm only twenty, and I don't think one could feel weaker at seventy. But all things come to an end, sometime, thank God!"

These words made Justine cringe, but she concealed her pain, not wishing to reveal as yet her true feelings for the Marquise.

It was time for the Marquise's dinner. The two old women came to advise Justine to get her into her room. The Marquise sat down and with a look of kindness and friendship invited Justine to sit and dine with her. There were at least twenty dishes on the table.

"As far as food is concerned I'm pretty well taken care of, you see."

"Yes," Justine answered, "I know that the Marquis wants you to be well taken care of."

"Oh yes, but knowing his motives, these attentions make little difference to me."

Constantly exhausted, the Marquise ate very much. After dinner she went to take an airing on the terrace. Justine supported her with one hand; without this help she could not have walked ten paces.

She showed Justine her arms, all covered with scars. "He doesn't stop there. There isn't a part from which he doesn't love to see the blood now." And she also showed her neck, her feet, all full of scars. They soon retired to bed.

The following day was the day for bleeding the Marquise. The Marquis, who set about this operation only on coming out from dinner, always taken before his wife's, told Justine to come and sit down at the table with him. It was here that she witnessed the usual routine of his enormous gluttony. Four valets served up this huge repast.

Several entrees were first served up; then a short rib of beef in the English fashion, eight side dishes, five courses of heavy meats, five lighter courses, and a wild boar's head in the middle of eight dishes of roast meats; which they took away in order to serve two courses of rich desserts and sixteen dishes of fruit, ices, six kinds of wine, four brands of liquor, and coffee. The Marquis ate of every dish. He drank twelve bottles of wine: four bottles of Burgundy on beginning the meal; four bottles of Champagne at the roast meats; the Tokai, Hermitage and Madeira were gulped down at dessert. He finished with two bottles of liquor from the Islands and ten cups of coffee.

As fresh on stepping up from the table as if he had just got out of bed, he said to Justine, "Come, let us now go and bleed your mistress. I want you to tell me if I go about it as well with her as I did with you."

Two young men whom Justine had not seen before were waiting for them at the door of the Marquise's apartment, where they all went in. Inside there were other young men. The Marquis had twelve of them, whom he changed every year.

The Marquise, dressed in a light gown, dropped to her knees as soon as her husband came in. "Are you ready?" he asked.

"For everything, sir," she humbly replied. "You know I can do nothing but obey you."

The Marquis then ordered Justine to bring his wife to him. The Marquise was fully acquainted with his procedure, and went through all the preliminaries of her own accord. In all these ceremonies the Marquis was abetted by his attendants.

Justine was greatly surprised that this huge man with such a frightening exterior was really, in spite of his bulk, so

92

small, hardly a man. But the evidence was before her eyes: like a three-year-old child's, the merest excrescence, barely the size of a peanut.

At last, his looks flashing fire, he pricked his wife with his lancet; but all these sores were light—one or two drops of blood hardly issued from them.

He sat down again and giving her a breathing spell, busied himself with two of his attendants. The Marquis received a great deal, but gave nothing in return; his satiety and impotence were such that the greatest efforts could not succeed in drawing him out of his numbness. There was really nothing to show for all the violence of his emotions.

He finally grabbed his wife again, and placed her as he had Justine, with her arms supported by two long ribbons attached to the ceiling. Justine was entrusted with the care of laying on the bindings. He inspected the bands, and not finding them tight enough he squeezed them tighter. He felt her veins and pricked them almost at the same time. The blood started to flow and he was happy. He was ten minutes in his delirium, struggling with himself like a man falling from epilepsy. Heaving cries that could have been heard a mile off and bellowing foul oaths, he struck at everything in his way. Two minions were upset. Exhausted, he got calm at last.

Justine immediately ran to the side of the Marquise, stopped the flow of blood, untied her, and took her to a sofa. She was terribly weak and exhausted. But the Marquis, without troubling himself, walked hastily out with his attendants and left it to Justine to put everything in order as she pleased.

Lying down, the Marquise told Justine that she had lost more blood than usual this time. But much care and many restoratives were lavished upon her.

Justine soon discovered the secret of getting into the Marquis' favor. He acknowledged that few women had pleased him so much. And so she acquired special privileges to his confidence.

One morning the Marquis called Justine into his room to discuss with her some new methods of bleeding. Listening very attentively to him, she applauded his ingeniousness. He was very calm and she wished to soften him regarding his wife. "How can you treat your own wife like that! Look how pretty she is!" she said.

"Oh, Therese, that's just what irritates me! Listen to me, dear girl," he went on, placing her near him, "whatever I say about your sex, don't be angry; I'll give you good reasons for it. By what logic do you think that a husband is obliged to make his wife happy? And what right has the wife to expect it? Only two persons of equal strength, equally capable of hurting each other, could be mutually happy together. And then, of course, on condition they both signed a pact to use their power to the injury of neither. But this happiness cannot exist between two people, one strong and the other weak. Why should the latter hope that the former would spare him, and why should the strong man deny himself the use of his power in return for nothing, for the sake of pity? This feeling is legitimate as I said before only between two persons of equal power. It is purely a selfish feeling. Its effect takes place on the tacit condition that the man who inspires me with mercy will have the same feeling for me. But if I have nothing to fear for him, his pity for me is useless and there is no reason why I should sacrifice myself by having any for him. Wouldn't I be a ninny to take pity on the chicken which is slaughtered for my dinner? Now a wife is just like a chicken. Both are household beasts to be used as designed by nature. I ask you, if it were nature's intention that our sex should be the happiness of yours and vice-versa, would this blind nature have made so many silly things in the construction of both of these sexes! Would she have wronged them so seriously that only estrangement and mutual antipathy could be the result! Take me for example. Therese, what woman could I make happy! And vice-versa, what man can find the enjoyment of a woman sweet unless he's supplied with the proportions, strength and great endurance necessary to satisfy her! I suppose you'll say that spiritual qualities will make up for these physical shortcomings. Hmm! What sane man on knowing a woman will not cry out with Euripides, 'He who of the Gods has placed woman in the world, may boast of having produced the worst of creatures, and the most troublesome for man!' So you see, the two sexes do not suit each other at all and it's false that nature created them for their reciprocal happiness. She may have created in them desire, merely for the sake of reproduction, but certainly not to find their happiness in each other. This happiness can only be found by woman's blind submission and absolute tyranny and oppression on the part of her master. Wasn't this nature's intention? Would she otherwise have made one inferior to the other in every respect! Isn't this fact sufficient indication it was nature's will that man use the power and right given him! We must not judge by the complaints of the feeble. Such a judgment would be vicious, narrow and feeble, since you borrow their ideas, which are forced upon them by their own unlucky fate. Action must be judged by the power of the strong, by the extent they give this power. When the effects of this power are extended to a woman, just observe what she is: a mean creature, in all ways inferior to man. She is less ingenious, less wise, wholly opposed to what can please man, to what can delight him: a sickly creature half of her lifetime. She is sour, peevish, haughty and has an infallible talent for nagging. A tyrant if entrusted with any power; low and crouching when dominated. Ever false, wicked and dangerous. In the Council of Macon it was seriously discussed whether this strange individual, so like a monkey, could pretend to the title of human creature and whether she could be reasonably called such. Just look at the way this despicable sex has always been looked upon by most people. Did the Medes, Persians, Babylonians, Greeks, Romans, Jews have any respect for her? Everywhere I see her crushed, everywhere rigorously removed from affairs, locked up. In short, treated like beasts, to be used in case of need and immediately put back into the fold. I hear the wise Cato crying out from the ancient capital of the world, 'If men were without women, they would converse with the Gods!' I hear a Roman Censor beginning his harangue with these words, 'Gentlemen, if it were possible for us to live without women, we should henceforth know true happiness.' I hear the poets singing in the theatres of Greece, 'O Jupiter! what reason could oblige thee to create women? Coulds't thou not bestow being on men by better, wiser ways, in fine, by means which would have spared us the plague of women!' These same nations held this sex in such contempt that laws were necessary to compel propagation, and one of their punishments was forcing a criminal to dress in woman's attire, namely to dress himself like the vilest and most contemptible creature they knew. But even in our own time I see women shut in throughout all Asia, serving there in slavery the barbarous whims of despots, who tease, torment them, and make a sport of their sufferings. In America I see nations naturally humane, the Eskimos, using among men all possible acts of benevolence, but treating women with incredible harshness. I behold them humiliated, prostituted to foreigners in one port of the universe and serving as money in another. In Africa, far more abased, they do the work of beasts of burden, ploughing the earth, sowing it, and waiting on their husbands only on their knees. In other islands they are beaten, tormented by their own children. Oh, Therese, let this not amaze you. Don't be so surprised at the universal right husbands had in all times over their wives. The nearer to nature people are, the better do they observe her laws. A wife has no other relation with her husband than a slave has with its master. She has no right to expect more. You must not confuse rights with ridiculous abuses, which, while debasing our sex, has for a time elevated yours. Let's find out the true cause of these abuses so that we may return to the wise counsel of reason. Now, Therese, here is the cause of that momentary respect which your sex got, and which still misleads those who prolong this respect. Among the Gauls of old, that part of the world only that did not wholly treat women as slaves, women were in the habit of prophesying, telling fortunes. It was imagined they were adept in this art because of their close communion with the Gods. Hence they were affiliated with the priesthood and enjoyed some of the consideration attached to priests. Upon these prejudices Knighthood was established in France, and finding women favorable to its spirit, honored them. But with this as with everything else: the causes died out and the effects were handed down. Knighthood disappeared and its prejudices remained. This ancient respect could not be done away with even when what was its cause had vanished: witches were no longer esteemed but prostitutes were venerated. What was worse, people continued to slaughter one another for them. It's about time we put a stop to such nonsense. Let it no longer influence the minds of philosophers. Let us put women back in their true place and use them as nature wills, as the wisest nations admit: mere individuals created for our pleasures, caprices; individuals whose weakness, trivialities and wickedness should deserve nothing but contempt! And, Therese, not only did all the nations enjoy the most expansive rights over their women, but there were some who even doomed them to death as soon as they were born. They conserved merely a small number requisite for reproduction of the specie; the Arabs, known under the name of Koreihs, used to bury daughters upon a mountain near Mecca. So vile a sex, they were wont to say, appeared to them unworthy of beholding the light of the day. In the seraglio of King Achem, the slightest suspicion of infidelity, the slightest disobedience in the service of the Prince's pleasures, or the moment they inspired disgust, brought them the most frightful tortures as punishment. On the banks of the Ganges they are compelled to immolate themselves over the ashes of their spouse, as being useless in the world, since their masters can no longer enjoy them. Elsewhere they are hunted down like wild beasts and it is an honor to kill them. In Egypt they are sacrificed to the Gods. At Formosa they are trampled under foot. The German laws used to condemn one who killed a strange woman only by a small fine; nothing if she happened to be his wife or his woman. Everywhere, I repeat, they are humiliated, oppressed, molested, sacrificed to the superstitions of priests or the cruelty of their husbands. And because I happen to live among a people still clownish enough not to abolish the most ridiculous prejudices, must I deprive myself of the rights nature gives me over this sex! No! no! Therese, it's not fair. I shall hide my behavior if necessary, but I shall make amends in silence. Because of these absurd views, the law condemns me to exile myself in my own retreat. There I'll treat my wife as I think fit, as I find in accord with universal codes, with my heart and nature!"

"Oh, sir!" Justine complained, "your conversation is impossible! It's hopeless to convert you!"

"Don't try it, Therese. The tree is too old to be bent. At my age one may go on a few steps farther in the career of evil, but not take a single one along the path of virtue. My principles and tastes have been my only happiness since childhood. They are the sole basis of all my conduct and actions. Further I can go on, but return, no! I have too much horror for men's prejudices. I hate their civilization, their sour, hypocritical virtues and their Gods too sincerely, ever to sacrifice any of my inclinations for them!"

Justine clearly saw that her only means of getting out of this house or freeing the Marquise was through craft and cunning.

During the year she had been near the Marquise she had often opened her heart to her and let it be seen how willing she was to help her. They had agreed on certain plans. The Marquise was to write to her mother telling of all the Marquis' infamies. She was sure her mother would at once come to her help. But they were so well locked in, so well kept within sight!

Accustomed to clearing walls, Justine surveyed those of the terrace. They were hardly thirty feet high. She thought that once at the bottom of these walls she had a clear way to the woods. She had discovered no enclosure blocking her way, but could not be certain of it. She decided to scale it. The Marquise wrote an effective, imploring letter to her mother, which Justine stuck inside her waist. As soon as it was dark, aided by a few sheets, she let herself down to the foot of the terrace. She was now in the park, but was greatly dismayed to find it surrounded by high walls, which the thickness of the trees had concealed. They were more than forty feet high, all protected on top. What was she going to do? Soon it would be getting light and her presence in the park would certainly arouse suspicion. How would she escape the Marquis' fury? He would drink down all her blood to punish her. It was impossible to return as the Marquise had already drawn in the sheets, and to knock on the door would more surely betray her.

Completely deprived of her will, in the darkness she crouched trembling with fear close to a tree. She knew the Marquis was pitiless, and was sure she was now doomed.

The high walls surrounding the park grew more and more clearly distinct in the vague gray of the morning. The first person she met was the Marquis himself. It was close and hot during the night and he was restless, rising very early to go out and take in the fresh morning air.

He stared at Justine and drew back, believing he was mistaken and what he saw was a ghost. Justine rose up, quivering, and dropped at his knees. "What are you doing here, Therese?"

"Oh, sir, punish me!" her voice shook tremulously. In the confusion or her fright she had forgotten to destroy the Marquise's letter hidden in her waist. He immediately sized up the entire situation and, conjecturing rightly, demanded she turn over the letter to him. She denied any such letter; but looking more closely he perceived it peering through the silk of her waist. He snatched it and quickly, greedily read it through.

He then ordered her to follow him. They went back into the castle by a hidden stairs-landing under the vaults.

After two or three turnings they stopped, and he opened the door of a dungeon and pitched her inside.

"Stupid bitch!" he snickered. "I warned you, didn't I? What you get you deserve! I'll settle with you tomorrow after supper!"

Again, from some irresistible compulsion of habit, she rushed at his knees, and begged for pity. But he grabbed her by her hair and after dragging her along the hard ground three or four times round the prison he dashed her head savagely against the wall.

"I'd like to open up all your veins!" he forced through his teeth. "I merely delay it to make it more horrible. Just wait, I'll show you what your virtue'll do for you!"

But Justine no longer heard him; she lay on the ground senseless. She passed a terrible night, in the most violent anxiety, and her head booming with pain and exhaustion.

She lay in this condition about thirty-six hours, when the door suddenly swung open and the Marquis strode in, alone. He had just got through wreaking his vengeance upon his wife. In his fury all his features seemed to have enlarged, his nose lumpier, eyes blacker, mouth and grin more formidable.

"I suppose you have some idea," he said, "of what I'm going to do to you. You're going to suffer all right! I'm going to make your blood flow from every pore in your skin! I'll bleed you three times a day; I want to see how long you can last. I was longing to make this experiment for some time. Thanks for giving me the chance."

And without bothering further he fell at once to pricking her arms, when one of the servants rushed in screaming, "Hurry sir.... hurry... your wife is dying... she wants to speak to you...."

He rushed out, forgetting in his sudden bewilderment to lock the door behind him. Despite her great debility, Justine had enough presence of mind to take advantage of the occasion, and she staggered through the door and got safely into the park. A door in the enclosure was unlocked, and she passed through unnoticed.

About nightfall she reached a hut some four miles from the castle. Hoping to reach Grenoble eventually, where she was sure some change of luck was waiting for her, she started out early next morning.

Chapter 15

ONE DAY WHILE glancing through a newspaper she was surprised to learn that Rodin, that surgeon of Saint Marcel who had so cruelly punished her for trying to prevent his murdering his daughter, Rosalie, had just been, according to the paper, appointed Head Surgeon to the Empress of Russia, with an enormous salary. "Good luck to him, the evil monster, so be it, since God wills it so!" she mumbled to herself. And in her thoughts she kept chewing upon the triumphs of vice and the misfortunes of virtue, when a note was handed to her by a strange lackey dressed all in gray.

He said that his master ordered him to wait for an answer. The note read:

A man who did you wrong, who thinks he recognized you in Bellecour-place, is longing to see you and make amends for his past conduct. Please come; he has good news to give you, which will clear him of all his obligations to you.

It was unsigned, and the lackey at first refused to give any further information. But Justine decided not to move unless the name of his master were made known to her.

"He is Mr. Florent, miss," the lackey finally said. "He said he had the honor of your acquaintance formerly in the suburbs of Paris, and that you did him a great service once which he would like to return. He's in a position to do it, too. He is one of the biggest business men in this town, and sure is rich. He is waiting for you impatiently."

She reflected a moment. If this man hadn't good intentions toward her, she thought, would he be likely to address her in this way? Maybe he had sincere remorse for his past actions; for having snatched from her of all possessions the one she had always held most dear. Yes, yes, he must have remorse and his conscience must bother him. She felt she really ought to help him. And could she not use his help, too! And then again he must be surrounded by fine, respectable people in whose presence he must have too much respect for himself to try anything funny with her. And would he not pity her! She made up her mind and told the lackey that she would have the honor of paying her respects to his master the next day about eleven.

She went into her room, and so taken up was she with what this man wanted to say to her that she slept very little all night.

The following morning she arrived at the address given her. It was a magnificent palace with a crowd of valets and attendants who looked down upon her with cold disdain. Disconcerted, she was about to withdraw, when the same lackey who delivered the note to her the night before came running out, and taking her encouragingly by the hand led her into a luxurious apartment. She was received by Florent, who was now a man getting on in years., Though it was some time since she had last seen him, she recognized him instantly. He was sitting in a huge armchair and did not rise. He beckoned Justine to a seat and ordered the lackey to leave them alone.

"I wanted to see you, my child," he said with a mortifying tone of superiority and superciliousness, "not because I'm under any obligation to you, but..."

"What, sir!—money that I gave you—the service I had done you—to be repaid by such conduct!"

"Ay, Therese, ay! But let me explain. You remember, don't you, that at first I just beat and plundered you? Well, I had already left you on the ground when about twenty feet away from you I began thinking of the pitiful state I left you in. This somehow got me excited. I was going away.... I retraced my steps and quickly finished the job. So you see how true it is that in certain natures voluptuousness springs up from crime. What am I saying?—crime alone arouses it. There is not a single passion it does not excite and improve."

"Oh, sir, how horrible!"

"At the time I could have done something worse. I confess to you I was very near it, but I figured you were already at your last extremity, and the thought of that satisfied me and so I left you. Let's pass over that and come to the point which made me wish to see you. That taste has not left me. The older one grows, in fact, the more pronounced become one's tastes. New crimes as well as old ones spring from fresh desires. All this, my dear, would be nothing, if what one employed as a means was not criminal in itself. But the consciousness of doing evil is what excites us. The greater the atrocity the greater our passion, and we like to sink deeper and deeper into the mire without wishing to get out of it. This is my confession to you, Therese: two girls are necessary every day for my sacrifices. The means of ridding myself of these victims are easy. An hour after having pleased me they are shipped and sold to pimps and bawds at Nimes, Montpelier, Toulouse, Aix, and Marseilles by my emissaries. This trade is very profitable to me and makes up for what they cost me. You see, I satisfy two of my dearest passions, lust and greed. But seeking out these girls and abducting them gives me a lot of trouble, as I am very particular about them. I like to seek them out of the slums, where poverty, hunger and misery sap all their courage, pride and delicacy. I have all those nooks carefully searched. You have no idea what a rich hoard the slums bring me. Sometimes I am forced to do a little maneuvering to keep this mine freshly supplied. With my influences in this town that's easy. I create by means of a few transactions a depression in trade, thereby increasing the unemployed, and, as a result, poverty. On the other hand, I limit the supply of necessary provisions and make them harder and more expensive to procure. Hunger and misery soon weaken all resistances to my schemes for delivering up my victims. It makes them easy prey. It's an old stunt, Therese. The same motives were behind the last famine we had in one of our largest towns. It is a complicated network, but the machine works smoothly and perfectly. But I want an intelligent, spruce young woman who has passed through the path of misery herself. Better than anybody else her experienced eyes would be able to ferret out misery in its most obscure garrets. She would recognize a prospect immediately. In short, a clever, efficient woman, unscrupulous and without pity, one who'd know her job. The last one I had was pretty good, but she died. I only wanted two subjects a day and she brought me six. God what a treasure she was! Now there's an opportunity for you, Therese. I think you'd make good. Five thousand francs a year for you, what do you say?"

"How dare you, sir! How could you be so pitiless! Have you no feelings for your fellow men!"

"That's all bosh! This is final, give me your answer. Take it or leave it!" he said.

"Never, never on my life, sir! As poor as I am, a thousand times, no!"

"Then take yourself off, slut," he very calmly said to her. "An indiscreet word out of your mouth and you'll be well taken care of, remember."

But in a sweeping spasm of rage something snapped inside of Justine and her usual timidity gave way and she flung out at him, "But how about the money you robbed me of in the Forest of Bondy? You have plenty of money now and I'm almost starving. Why don't you give it back to me now?"

"You can earn it if you want to, it all depends on yourself."

"No! A thousand times, no!" she firmly replied. "I'd sooner die!"

"And I, too, would sooner die than give my money away without it being earned. Do you think I find my money in the streets! Now, listen, I'll still give you a little of my time, in spite of the fact you've had the nerve to refuse me. Come into my study a minute and we'll set matters right. Just a little obedience and you'll get your money."

"Keep your money, skinflint. I don't intend to give you that enjoyment. I'm not a whore and am not asking for alms. I merely want what you owe me!" she spoke rapidly with unusual defiance. She was carried away, barely aware of her own presence.

But Florent was already shoving her into the door of his private study. She put up such a resistance, however, that with much disgust he gripped her arm and dragged her across the room; and giving her a savage box on the ear, threw her out into the hallway. He was that lenient toward her only because they were already waiting to bring in one of his daily victims.

Chapter 16

SHE LEFT LYONS the next day. Her heart still set on Grenoble, that fine town which was the great hope of her weary soul, she went by way of Dauphiny.

As usual, she set out on foot, with just a handful of her personal belongings tucked under her arms.

It was a bright clear day, and the air so soft and golden with sunlight that only a short distance out, all her troubles, and Lyons with all its miseries, were things of the past, remote and forgotten. It's still God's world, she thought, tears of tenderness and joy welling up into her eyes.

About two miles out an old woman, with a look of suffering, accosted her and besought her for alms. Justine's heart was greatly moved and she took out her purse to give her a coin. But the old woman, so decrepit and broken down, was surprisingly quick, and with one movement snatched the purse out of Justine's hand, and in another gave her a wicked poke in the belly that laid her low.

When Justine came to, all her courage and hope forsook her and she was bitter. In this world, she thought, it was impossible to open your soul to a virtuous deed without being rebuffed for it. And despair, like an evil genius, crept into her soul. She was ready to quit the career in which she was pricked with so many thorns and return to Lyons and accept the proposals of Florent. But almost the same instant remorse for her thoughts overtook her, and she fell to her knees and thanked God for sparing and sustaining her from yielding to temptation.

Her ill-fated star, she thought, could only lead her, though innocent, to want, hunger, and misery, but not to the gallows and disgrace, not to the choice of an evil life.

She continued on toward the town of Vienne, there hoping

to sell, in order to reach Grenoble, what she had left.

Walking slowly along, sad and pensive, she got to about a quarter of a mile out of the town of Vienne, when she saw in the plain, on the right side of the road, two men trampling another under their horses' hoofs, and then gallop off at full speed, leaving him behind apparently dead.

Such a scene greatly affected her. And it struck her that there was a man more to be pitied than herself, who at least had health and strength left.

Compassion soon got the upper hand of her feelings and she could not overcome the impulse of going up to this man and helping him.

She ran to his side. She lifted his head, moistened his lips with water and gave him some to drink. Lavishing great care and attention upon him she soon made his breathing much easier. She then tore up one of her chemises and stanched the blood coming from some of his bruises. As he was not at all seriously injured he soon opened his eyes and staggered to his feet.

He seemed to be a man of some distinction, and well dressed, though his clothes were all torn and grimy with dust.

When his wind came back to him he asked Justine who was the kind angel that brought him such care and assistance and what he could do for her to show his gratitude. She acknowledged his thanks with tears, and soon they were both shedding them mutually in each other's arms. The tenderness of this scene loosened her tongue and she began telling this strange man all her misfortunes. He was interested and much moved. "My name is Roland," he said. "I have a fine house in the mountains a long way from here. Why don't you come with me? This invitation doesn't sound delicate, but let me explain. You see, I am a bachelor and live with a sister to whom I'm devoted. She needs a companion and I want somebody to look after her. She'd like you very much. Why don't you come?"

She thanked him warmly for such a generous offer of help and protection and they set out.

Chapter 17

ON THE WAY he said, "I feel much better now, thanks to you."

Justine then took the liberty of asking him how a rich man such as he travelled without attendants and exposed himself to the danger of being attacked, as had just happened to him.

"I'm young and pretty strong and have always travelled this way alone, on business. I've never been molested before. If I take no one with me it's not because of the expense; I'm rich, as you'll soon see for yourself, and money doesn't bother me; but I enjoy travelling alone better. Those two men who just knocked me down are two shabby gents of this district from whom I won some money last week in a gambling house at Vienne. They promised to pay me and I was satisfied with their word of honor and met them today and that was how they paid me off. But," he said, "it'll be soon getting dark; we'd better hurry. I know a place about two miles from here where we can stop overnight. Tomorrow we'll get fresh horses there and be able to reach home the same evening."

Quickening their pace, they did finally reach the inn he mentioned.

They had supper pleasantly together. Later he recommended Justine to the care of the mistress of the house and they both retired separately. She had never felt so happy.

The next morning on two hired mules, escorted by the valet of the inn, they reached the borders of Dauphiny, still steering their course toward the mountains.

The journey being too long to make in one day, they pulled up at Virieu, where Justine received the same cares, the same consideration from her new master. They continued on their way the following day.

About four in the afternoon they got to the foot of the mountains. There the road became almost impassable and Roland, fearing some mishap, charged the muleteer not to leave Justine. They penetrated deep into the narrow passages. The road curved so continuously, rising and descending, that after travelling about four miles, with every beaten track and sign of life behind them, Justine fancied she was at the end of the world.

In spite of herself, a little uneasiness started to come over her which Roland could not help noticing; but he said nothing. His silence made her even more uneasy.

At last they beheld a castle, perched on top of a mountain at the brink of a deep precipice, into which it seemed ready to sink. No road leading to it appeared and they had to follow a goat-path, cluttered with stones on all sides.

"There's my house," said Roland. '

Justine expressed her surprise that he lived in such a wild, desolate place.

"It suits me!" he answered.

This reply redoubled her fears, so much indeed that she now hung upon his every word, gesture and shade of tone to find some reassurance for her growing anxiety. She could do nothing else, and kept silent.

About a quarter of a mile from the castle Roland alighted from his mule and got Justine to do the same. He handed both mules to the muleteer, paid him and ordered him to return.

His procedure gave Justine a great deal of fresh worriment. Roland was aware of it and said, "What ails you, Therese? You're not out of France. We're on the border of Dauphiny and very near Grenoble."

"I know," she answered, "but what makes you settle down in a place like this?"

"Because those who live in it are very honest folk, that's

why. Maybe you'll learn something!"

"Ah, sir!" she said to him, "how you frighten me! Where are you taking me?"

"Nowhere—just a gang of counterfeiters." He grabbed her arm and forced her to cross a little bridge which was lowered at their arrival and raised again immediately after.

As soon as they had entered he showed her a deep grotto at the bottom of the yard, where four chained women were making a wheel turn. "Do you see this well," he said, "there are your companions, and that'll be your job. Provided you work ten hours daily, turning this wheel, and satisfy us like those women, you'll be allowed black bread and a plate of beans every day. As for your freedom, forget about it—you haven't a chance! When you're old and worn out you'll be thrown into that hole there alongside of the well, with about sixty others like you waiting for you inside of it—and then we'll get somebody to replace you."

"Oh God, please!" she cried, throwing herself at his feet, "remember how I saved you.... You promised to make me happy and protect me... how can you forget what I did for you?"

"What do you mean 'What I did for you'!" he said. "Why, you bitch, what were you doing when you came to help me—wasn't it to satisfy an impulse of your own heart! Didn't satisfying it give you pleasure! How in hell can you ask me to be grateful to you for the pleasures you give yourself! And what makes you think that a man like myself, floating in wealth, can owe you anything—a slut like you! If you saved me you did it to satisfy and enjoy your own sentiment—I owe you nothing.... To work, slave, to work!"

He gave her no time for further delay and ordered two attendants to strip and chain her with the rest. She had to get right to work, without being permitted to rest herself after the tiresome journey she had just made.

Many hours later Roland approached her and making her

stop in her tracks, chained to the wheel, forced her to listen to him as he sat himself comfortably down.

"I want you to know, Therese," he said, "that civilization in overthrowing the principles of nature still leaves the latter some rights, however. In the beginning, you know, nature created strong and weak beings. She intended that the weak be subordinated to the strong. But the dexterity, the intelligence of man diversified the position of individuals; it was no longer physical force that determined ranks, it was money. The richest man became the strongest; the poorest, the weakest. So you see, as long as the priority of power is established, nature is indifferent to whether it be the weak or the poor who are crushed by the man of riches, or the man of strength. Now as for the feeling of gratitude you claim I owe you, it was never nature's intention that one who received a favor should forego his rights over the other who yielded to the pleasure of obliging him. Do you find such sentiments among animals? The pride of an elevated soul should never allow itself to be bowed down by an obligation. Is not he who receives always humiliated? And does not this humiliation which he feels, sufficiently pay the benefactor, who by that alone finds himself raised above the other? Is it not an enjoyment for pride, to raise oneself above the other? Does he who obliges need any other? And if the obligation, in humbling him who receives, becomes a burden to him, why force him to keep it? Why must I allow myself to be humiliated every time one who has obliged me looks at me! Ingratitude, therefore, instead of being a vice, is really the virtue of proud souls, just as expecting gratitude is that of weak souls. Let people oblige me as much as they like, but let them ask nothing in return for having enjoyed the sentiment of obliging."

He then armed himself with a bull's pizzle and saluted her with twenty stripes. He said, "I don't do this, Therese, for any fault already committed by you, but merely to give you

111

an idea how I act when you do. This is just how you'll be dealt with when you are lax in your duties."

He greeted her tears with light mockery. "Ah," he said, "I shall hear more of them; your troubles are first beginning." And he left her.

Their time was up and Justine as well as her companions were untied. After having been given their daily portion of water, bread and beans, they were locked in for the night.

Under a grotto round this vast well there were six small dark cells, which were locked up like dungeons. There the girls spent the night.

Justine was lost in sombre reflection when the door of her cell was opened and in walked Roland, who seemed nervous and irritable. He gazed at Justine a moment with eyes that made her start.

"Follow me!" he said.

And he got hold of her by the arm and dragged her along. He led her with his right hand, and with his left held a small lantern which dimly lighted their way. After several turnings they got to the door of a cave. He opened it and forcing her in first, told her to descend while he locked the door behind. Much farther on they met a second one which was opened and shut the same way. But when they got into the second cave there were no steps, but a narrow road which, curving around, kept going down.

They walked along about twenty minutes, the sickly blur of light from his lantern occasionally lighting up in the damp stone walls niches containing huge chests of money.

He was silent all the way.

They had got far down into the bowels of the earth. At last they came to a bronze gate which opened into a large round vault about thirty feet in diameter. It was a dark dismal place, furnished with black hangings, and on the walls skeletons of every size, bones formed crosswise, leering death-heads, rods, whips, switches, daggers and pistols. A

112

lamp was suspended from one of the corners of the vault, and in the center a long rope fell to about ten feet above the ground. On the right stood a coffin, with a kneeling desk alongside, above which hung a crucifix placed between two large black candles. On the left fastened to a cross there was a wax effigy of a naked woman, so real and lifelike that for some time Justine was actually deceived by it. It was nailed to the cross breastwise, so that all its hind parts were clearly exposed. The flesh seemed horribly mortified, and the blood oozed, dripping down along the thighs. Covered with fine hair, its head was turned, appearing to implore forgiveness. All the contorted expressions of suffering on its face seemed so real, even the tears flowing from the protruding, blood-stained eyes. The end of the vault was taken up by a vast black sofa.

"If you ever get the idea into your head to get away, here's where you'll meet your finish!" Roland said. And merely making this threat inflamed him and made him twitch.

Molesting her furiously, he told her that since he now held her in this den it was just as well she didn't leave it, which would save him the trouble of bringing her all the way down again.

She rushed to his knees and tried to remind him again of the good turn she had done him. This irritated him still further and he ordered her to hold her tongue, knocking her down upon the floor with a blow of his knee.

"Come!" he said, hauling her up by the hair, "come, get ready! I'm certainly going to sacrifice you now!"

"Master... master...!"

"No, no! you must die! I'm sick of hearing myself reproached with your trifling favors; I like to owe nothing to anybody! You must die, I tell you... get into this coffin, see if it fits you!"

He flung her into it, locked her in, then went out of the vault, pretending he was leaving her there. But he soon came back and took her out.

"You look swell in there!" he said. "It was just made for you. But to let you die quietly in there would be too fine a death. I have a better one for you, not half so comfortable. Come, wench, implore your God! Beg him to come and save you; if he really has the power of doing it!"

She threw herself upon the kneeling stool, and while in a loud voice she poured out her heart to the Eternal, Roland tortured her still more cruelly. He scourged her with a hammer studded with steel spikes, every blow of which forced the blood to spurt and spatter into his face. And he continued raving, "Well! your prayers don't help you! Your unhappy virtue only makes you suffer! It gives way before the hands of wickedness... oh, what a delicious irony that is, Therese! Come, your prayer must be over!"

He set her on the sofa again. "You must die, Therese, I told you so, didn't I!"

He gripped her arms and, tying them to her legs, passed round her neck a black silk cord, both ends of which he held in his hands. At will, he was able to tighten the cord around her neck and choke her to death.

"This torture, Therese," he said, "is sweeter than you think. You will feel death through exquisite sensations of pleasure. The squeezing that this cord effects upon the mass of your nerves, will set you on fire. If all persons condemned to this torture knew in what intoxication it brings death they would be less frightened by this punishment and commit their crimes oftener and with far more assurance. This delightful operation, Therese," he continued, "will just about redouble my own pleasure too!"

His fury knew no bounds. The more he succeeded, the tighter he pulled the cord round her neck. This amused him and he egged her on to yell louder and louder, modulating the pressure of the cord according to the degree of his pleasure. Then all at once he pulled so violently that the color in

114

Justine's face turned blue and her senses slowly slipped from under her and her voice gradually died out.

When she opened her eyes she found herself unbound, and he said to her, "Well, Therese, tell me the truth, didn't you get any pleasure out of it! It doesn't matter; I'm worried more about my own pleasure. It was so good that I'm going to try it again in just a few moments."

Raising her up on a stool, he threw round her neck the rope hanging from the ceiling, and firmly fastened it. He then tied a cord to the stool, and holding the end, sat down in an armchair opposite. He had given Justine a sharp knife with which she was to cut the rope hanging above her just at that moment when by means of the cord he pulled the stool from under her feet.

"Therese," he said, "it all depends on yourself. If you miss your aim I certainly shall not miss mine. Am I wrong in telling you your life depends on yourself?"

He sat down and intended to pull the stool away the moment he reached the high moment of his intoxication.

He was in his full glory and, teasing Justine's already over-strained nerves, often made a feint at pulling the stool. But soon the violence of his feelings betrayed him into making the fatal movement; the stool slipped away, she cut the rope and fell safely to the ground.

The knife in her hand, she might have taken him by surprise and rushed upon him; but she knew it would be useless. She hadn't the keys and, not knowing the way, she would have been dead before she got half-way out of this hidden catacomb. Moreover, he was always armed.

Pleased with her mildness and quite satisfied, he beckoned her to go out, and they both went upstairs again.

Chapter 18

NEXT DAY JUSTINE examined her companions more closely. The four girls with her were all from about twenty-five to thirty years old. Though stupefied by misery and deformed by their severe labor they still retained a few relics of their former beauty. They were all well built, and the youngest, Suzanne, was especially lovely, with fine eyes and very pretty hair. Roland had taken her at Lyons and carried her away to this castle about three years ago. She more than the others suffered Roland's ferocities. By dint of being lashed with the bull's pizzle her buttocks had become as callous and hard as a cow's hide dried in the sun.

It was she who informed Justine that Roland was soon to set out for Venice, if the large sums he lately had gotten passed in Spain returned him the bills of exchange he was awaiting in Italy. He did not like to carry his gold beyond the mountains, and never sent any there; and was wont to get his forged monies passed in a different country from the one in which he wished to settle down. By this means, rich with the bills of another country, he could never be found out. But any minute everything might go wrong, and the retreat he was contemplating depended on this last transaction in which the principal amount of his treasures was at stake. If his *piasters, zechins* and *louts* were accepted at Cadiz and he got, accordingly, bills of Venice, Roland would be happy for the rest of his life. But if his fraud were discovered, one day alone would suffice to ruin him.

"Great god!" cried Justine, "I hope they get him!"

About twelve o'clock the girls were allowed two hours' rest, by which they generally profited going singly to their rooms to eat and breathe and relax. But at two they were tied up again and forced to work until night.

They were mostly naked not only because of the heat, but much rather to be in a better way of receiving the stripes of the bull's pizzle which their master came occasionally to lay on. In cold weather they were supplied with a pair of trousers and waistcoat so tight to the skin that their bodies were nevertheless just as well exposed to the blows of a man whose pleasure was to thrash them.

That same night, Roland came again for Justine in her dungeon, and, falling into a passion at the sight of his cruelties, started to molest and abuse her again. When he appeared assuaged, she took advantage of his moment's calmness and entreated him to ease her lot. But, alas, she was still not aware that if in such natures the moment of delirium renders their passion for cruelty more active, calmness does not on the other hand soften them; or that they are possessed by a fire, even though under ashes, which burns nevertheless at all times, because of an inextinguishable supply of fuel constantly keeping it up.

"And why should I?" he answered. "By what right do you ask that I ease your lot? Is it because of the pleasure you have given me? But am I going at your feet begging for the favors you grant me? I ask nothing from you—I take. I do not see why, because I use a right over you, I must abstain from exacting a second one. There is no love in my case. Love is a chivalrous sentiment thoroughly despised by me, and my heart has never felt it. I make use of a woman from necessity as one makes use of a round hollow vase in a different need. But I never bestow either esteem or tenderness upon an individual whom my money or strength submits to my passions. I owe only to myself for what I rob. Never requiring submission, why should I show gratitude? Does a man who steals another's purse owe him any thanks? It is the same with a crime committed on a woman. There's always good cause to commit a second one, but never sufficient reason for making amends." He was a very outspoken I man.

"Oh, sir! to what height you carry wickedness!"

"To the highest point, Therese, to the highest point! [There isn't anything I have not given way to, nothing that I have not done I My principles excuse and make legitimate every one of them. I have always found in evil an attraction.

117

Crime, kindles my lust, and the more I frightful it is the more it excites me. I enjoy in committing it the same kind of pleasure ordinary people I taste in a woman—even more, much more. On a thousand occasions when I've found myself thinking of crime—giving myself up to it, or having just committed it—it put me in the same state as one is when beside a lovely naked woman; it stirs my senses up in the same way. I perpetrate it in order to be inflamed. Without it I am impotent."

"Oh, sir! what you say is awful, but I have seen examples of it before."

"There are a thousand of them, Therese. You must not imagine that it is a woman's beauty which stirs up the spirit. It is really the crime involved that makes possession attractive to me. The more criminal, the more, inflamed one is. The man who enjoys a woman he steals from her husband, a girl he seduces, is undoubtedly far more delighted than the husband who merely enjoys his wife. And the more worthy of respect the bonds severed, the more delightful is the act. When one has tasted all, he wants his obstacles increased in order to cause pains and have greater difficulty surmounting them. Now, if crime seasons an enjoyment, separate from this enjoyment, it can be a pleasure in itself. Yes, crime alone can be an enjoyment. Otherwise, how could it lend savor if it weren't itself savory. These theories lead far, I know. I'll even prove it to you before long just how far. But it doesn't matter, as long as one enjoys. Was there, for instance, my child, anything simpler or more natural than to see me enjoy you? You didn't think so. You thought I was under an obligation to you. But I yield to nothing; I break all the ties which ensnare fools. I subject you to my desires, and out of the simplest, the most monotonous enjoyment I make a truly delightful one. Yield therefore, Therese, yield and learn. When you return to the world as one of the strong, misuse likewise your rights and you shall see how lively and acute every pleasure will be!"

Roland walked out and left her absorbed in bitter reflections.

Chapter 19

JUSTINE HAD already been in this den about six months, serving all Roland's whims, when one evening he walked into her cell with Suzanne.

"Come, Therese," he said, "it seems to me a long time since I've taken you down to that vault which had frightened you so much. Follow me, both of you; but don't you both expect to come back; I must leave one behind—we'll see to whose lot it'll fall."

Justine stood up and cast bewildered looks as Suzanne, whose eyes were clouded with tears. They went down.

Hardly were they shut up in the underground vault when Roland gloated over them with wild eyes. He took special pleasure in repeating their doom, and in convincing them that one of the two would certainly remain behind.

"Come," he said, seating himself and making them stand straight up before him, "she who pleases me best will get the prize."

"It's not right," said Suzanne, "she who pleases you best ought to be the one to be forgiven."

"Not at all! The moment I find out who is best, I will be certain then that *her* death will give me most pleasure. Besides, if I were to pardon the one who pleased me, the more you'd both set to work with such ardor that you would perhaps cast my senses into the ecstasy before the complete consummation of the sacrifice, and this is just what I don't want."

"The completion of your ecstasy is all you should want, and if you attain it without crime, why must you commit one!" said Justine.

"Ah! because I shall reach it more deliciously, and I came

down here to commit one, and commit one I'm going to! That lovely skin, Therese," he said to Justine, "is still very far from being as hard and callous as Suzanne's. One could set fire to that dear girl's rumps and she would not feel it. But yours, Therese, but yours..."

This threat really tranquillized her. Since he intended to subject her to fresh cruelties it was obvious to her that he had not as yet a mind to immolate her.

"I don't think," he said to Suzanne, "that the most frightful lashes could draw another drop of blood from that back of yours!"

He frisked about, as animated as a young colt in spring.

"Suzanne," he said at last, "you win. I don't know what I should like to do to you!"

"Oh, sir, have pity on her, she is in enough pain!" Justine pleaded.

"Oh, yes! Ah, if I only had that famous Emperor Kie here we should indeed do something different. I am too mild, Therese, quite a stranger to it all, a mere school boy!"

"Come, Therese," he said, "come, dear girl, let's have a little game of rope cutting."

She got upon the stool with the rope round her neck. He set himself before her and Suzanne attended him. Armed with the knife, Justine cut it at just the right moment and fell to the ground without any harm.

"All right," said Roland, "it is your turn, Suzanne. Good luck to you if you get out of it with as much skill!"

And so she was next raised up on the tripod. But her he hung.

"Let's go out, Therese, you'll not come back here again until your turn comes."

The next day her companions asked Justine what had become of Suzanne. She told them and they were not at all surprised. It seemed they were all awaiting the same doom, and even eagerly desired it.

At last tidings were spread through the castle that Roland not only received the immense quantity of bills he had requested for Venice, but that he was also asked for another six million of forged money.

Such were the new state of things when Roland went to Justine to take her down for the third time to the underground vault. Recalling the threats he made her the last time they were there, she was tense with anxiety.

"Cheer up, Therese," he said, "you have nothing to fear—it's about something concerning myself, a strange sensation I wish to enjoy; but it will make you run no risk."

She followed him down, and as soon as the door was shut he said, "Therese, you're the only one in the house whom I could rely on. I prefer you even to my sister."

She was filled with surprise and asked him to explain himself.

"Listen," he said, "my fortune is made, but at any time I may be ruined. I may be watched and they may grab me during the conveyance I'm going to make of my riches. If that happens, the rope'll be my end. As punishment they'll give me the same pleasure I delight in making women taste. Now, I'm convinced that this death is much more mild than cruel. But as the women whom I made feel its first pangs were never really truthful with me, I want ,to find out for myself its sensation. I want to have it tried on my own person, and know from my own experience if the squeezing does not really bring on pleasure. Once persuaded that this death is but a pastime, I shall more easily face in when my time comes. It is not that I am afraid of death—I no more fear hell than I expect paradise; but I should not like to suffer while dying. So let's try it, Therese. You will do everything to me that I did to you. I am going to strip and get up on this stool; you will fasten the rope and I'll excite myself. As soon as you see that I'm about getting ready you'll pull away the stool, and let me hang for a while. You'll let me hang until you see my pleasure complete, or notice symptoms of suffering. In the second case you will set me loose at once, but in the first case you will let nature take its full course and loose me only afterwards. You see, Therese, I put my life in your hands. Your freedom, fortune, will be the price of your good conduct."

"Ah, sir," said Justine, "it's an extravagant proposal!"

"No, Therese, you must!" he answered, undressing. "But behave well. See what proof I give you of my confidence and esteem."

What would have been the good of her wavering—was he not master of her?

He got upon the stool, the rope round his neck, and wanted Justine to rail at him, curse him with all the horrors of his life, all which she did. He got ready and beckoned her to pull away the stool.

Hanging by his neck for a while, his tongue was lolling half way out, his eyes bulging; but soon, beginning to swoon away, he motioned feebly to Justine to set him loose.

On being revived he said, "Oh Therese! one has no idea of such sensations, what a feeling! It surpasses anything I know! Now they can hang me if they want! But, Therese, again you're going to find me very graceless. But what can I do, my dear—people do not correct themselves at my age. You dear creature, you have just given me my life, and never was I so bent on taking yours. You complained of Suzanne's fate, well, I'm going to have you join her. I am going to throw you alive into that hole she's buried in."

He dragged her, screaming, to a huge cylindrical hole concealed in a far corner of the vault. He opened the lid and lowered a lamp into it so that she could better distinguish the host of dead bodies with which it was lied. He then slipped a long rope under her arms, which were tied behind her back, and let her down about thirty feet into the hole, half-way to the bottom. In this condition she suffered frightfully, and it seemed to her that her arms were being pulled from their sockets. The loathsome smell almost stifling her, she thought she was about to end her days in midst of the heap of dead bodies. And way above her she heard him raving with delirium and threatening to cut the rope. However, he merely took pleasure in threatening, but didn't really do it, and after some time drew her up again.

"Were you afraid, Therese?"

"Oh, sir! oh.... oh!"

"That's how you'll die, Therese, be sure of it!" he said. "I just want you to get used to it!"

At last Roland was ready to take his leave. On the eve of his departure he went in to see Justine to pay her his last respects.

She threw herself at his feet and begged him to set her free, and to give her a little money to get to Grenoble.

"To Grenoble? Certainly not, you would squeal on us there."

"Well, kind sir," she implored with tears, "I promise you never to go there. To convince you of it take me as far as Venice. I swear never to give you any trouble!"

"I won't give you a franc!" he replied. "Pity and gratitude, as I told you a thousand times already, is not in me, and were I three times as rich as I am, I wouldn't give any poor man a sou. The sight of misfortune only excites me, amuses me. These are principles I never turn from, Therese,—I told you. Poverty is a natural thing, and it was nature's intention that civilization should not change this primary law. To relieve the needy man is to destroy the order of nature and overthrow that balance which is the basis of her most sublime arrangements; it is to teach indolence and slothfulness, it is to teach the poor an equality dangerous to society!"

"Oh, sir, would you speak like that if you were not rich?"

"That may be, Therese. Everyone has his own way of seeing things; such is mine and I shall not change it. People complain of the beggars in France. If they wanted to, they could hang seven or eight thousand of them and they'd all be gone. Would a man devoured by vermin allow them to live upon him through pity? Why act differently in this case?"

"But virtue!" Justine cried, "benevolence! Humanity!"

"They are stumbling blocks to happiness. If I have made myself happy it's mostly because I have rid myself of all the stupid prejudices of men. I have mocked divine and human laws and always sacrificed the weak man when I found him in my way. In cheating the public, gullible as they are, in ruining the poor man and robbing the rich, I have arrived where I am. Why didn't you do as I did; you had the same opportunity. But you preferred imaginary and fantastic virtues instead—was it worth while? But it's too late, Therese, too late—weep for your faults, it's all you can do."

And finishing this conversation, again he forced her to stoop to his aberrant desires and whims, almost strangling her. When he felt thoroughly allayed, he took out the bull's pizzle and branded her body with lash upon lash; and he told her she had good cause to be happy, as he had not enough time to give her more of them.

The next day before actually setting out he had a farewell scene of fresh atrocities. Roland was an avid reader of the Roman historians, and some of his methods of torture and ferocity he slavishly borrowed from the annals of Nero, Andronicus and Tiberius.

It was thought that Roland's sister would leave with him, as he had taken her out of the castle fully dressed. But before mounting his horse he ordered her to take her post alongside of the other women and said, "My comrades think I was smitten with this slut; but I'll leave her behind as a pledge. Since I'm going to take such a dangerous trip I might as well try out my pistols on one of these bitches—

there are more here than are wanted, anyway."

And he loaded one of his pistols and stuck it into the I breast of every one of the girls lined up before him, but only when he reached his sister, who was last in line, did he discharge it.

She did not instantly expire but struggled for a long while under her chains.

On the day after Roland's departure everything changed. His successor was a mild and reasonable man and had the girls instantly released from their chains and labor.

"That is no work for women," he kindly said to them. "The trade we carry on is bad enough without making it worse by such terrible things."

Instead they were all given work in the castle, cutting the coins and stamping them, work which wasn't really very hard, and for their labor were given good rooms and excellent food.

At the end of about two months Dalville, Roland's successor, informed the girls of the safe arrival of his colleague.

It was now quiet and nice at the castle, and under the kind, new master the work, though criminal, went on smoothly and merrily.

But one day the doors were suddenly broken in, the fences scaled and the house filled, before the men had time to think of their defense, with a battalion of soldiers. There was nothing to do but surrender. They were all chained like beasts, tied upon horses and conveyed to Grenoble.

The case of the counterfeiters was soon tried. When the brand on Justine's shoulder was seen, they almost spared themselves the trouble of questioning her, and she was about to be condemned to the fate of the others, to be hung, when she obtained some pity from one of the magistrates, who was the most influential man of this tribunal, an upright judge and a man celebrated for his good sense and kindliness. He listened attentively to her and was convinced by her manner of her good faith and the truth of her misfortunes. He himself pleaded for her, and because of his power and influence she was found innocent, though misled; and was given her full liberty. Her protector even took up a small collection for her. She thought her troubles were now at last over and wept for sheer joy.

Chapter 20

JUSTINE HAD gone to live near the suburbs in an inn facing the water. Following the advice of the man who got her her freedom, it was her intention to stay there for some time and try to get work in town; but if she did not succeed, to return to Lyons with letters of recommendation from her influential protector.

The second day at the inn, while having her lunch in the dining room, she noticed that she was being closely watched by a stout, well dressed woman sitting at a nearby table, who had herself styled, *Baroness.*

Justine looked more closely at the woman and wondered where she had seen her before; and then they caught each other's eye and both started to stare, trying to place one another. The Baroness finally rose, came over to Justine's table and, very gracious, asked was she mistaken—was it not Therese she was speaking to, the same Therese she rescued ten years ago from jail;—did she not recall La Dubois?

Justine was little flattered by this discovery, but answered her politely, being aware that she had to do with a clever, crafty woman.

Madame Dubois loaded her with courtesy and attentions. She said that she had been worried about Justine's recent scrape with the authorities, but that she had learned of it too late; she would otherwise have gotten in touch with the magistrates, among whom were some of her bosom friends.

Feeble as usual, Justine allowed herself to be led on in this way, and Madame Dubois easily ingratiated herself. Justine was soon telling her all the misfortunes she experienced since their last meeting.

"My dear friend," Madame Dubois said, embracing her, "I'm so sorry to hear it. I've wanted to see you so long, Therese! But everything will be all right now. I have lots for both of us. Look," showing her hands, covered with glittering diamonds. "That's the result of my profession. You see, Therese, if I had been virtuous like you, today I'd be locked in jail or hung!"

"Oh, madame!" Justine answered, "if you got all that through crime, it won't always last. Providence always punishes evil in the end!"

"You're mistaken, Therese. Don't think that providence always befriends virtue. Don't let the good luck you're running in now for a little while lead you astray. It is all one to providence whether Paul does evil or Peter good. Nature requires both, and crime even more than virtue is the most indifferent thing in the world to her. Listen, Therese!" as she bent over closer to her, "you're intelligent, my child, and I'd like to convince you, really! It is not a question of *choosing* between virtue and vice; that doesn't make a man happy— both are simply ways of conducting oneself. But what makes a man happy is to do as everybody else—that's what counts. He who doesn't follow the mob is always wrong, in a wholly virtuous world I would recommend virtue to you, because then only virtue would be rewarded, and happiness would depend completely upon just that. But in a wholly corrupted world like ours, vice is the only thing. He who does not fall in with the rest hasn't a chance; everybody steps all over him—he is weak and hopelessly crushed. The laws vainly try to talk virtue to the mass, but it's just talk. The people who make the laws are really too biased towards evil and never carry out their fine talk—they merely make a stab at it for the sake of appearances, that's all. These same men who are always in power realize the advantage of vice and unscrupulous-ness and wish everybody else to be virtuous so that they alone might have the greater benefit of this advantage, and get the upper hand. Can't you see that corruption is the general interest of men—that he who will not be corrupted with them struggles against the general interest? Now what happiness can a man expect who thwarts the interest of others? I suppose you'll tell me that it is vice which is opposed to men's interest. That's true, I admit, in a world composed of an equal share of good and bad people, because then the interest of the one would evidently clash with the interest of the other. But that doesn't hold in a wholly corrupted society such as ours, where one's vices could only wrong the wicked; but who in turn are given the opportunity of other vices which indemnify them; and so they all find themselves happy. It is a mutual exchange of injuries, one compensating for the other. Vice only hurts virtue, which really shouldn't exist; and when it no longer exists, vice can hurt only the wicked, but no longer virtue itself. Then it will be just vice pitted against vice; and instead of hurting each other they will merely stimulate one another. Do you see, dear child, what I'm driving at? It's no wonder that you have failed a thousand times in your life—taking every road but the one everybody was following. If you had followed the general current you would have been as well off and happy as I am now. Is it as easy going up a river as down it? Another thing, you're always talking to me about providence, that it loves order, and virtue. Isn't it constantly giving you examples of its injustices and irregularities,—sending men war, famine, plagues, floods and earthquakes? Isn't it a universe vicious in all its parts and ways? Is that your idea of a providence loving virtue! Why do you insist that vicious individuals displease it, since it acts itself only through vices, since all is evil and corruption in its works, since all is crime and disorder in its will! Moreover, Therese, from whom do our passions for evil come if not from its own hand? Isn't that the work of providence too! A little more philosophy in the world would soon set everything right, and judges and legislators would soon see that the crimes they blame and punish in others but not in themselves, is far more useful sometimes than those virtues they preach; but which they never reward; or practice themselves."

"But supposing that I adopted your theories," said Justine, "how about my conscience—wouldn't I suffer from remorse almost every minute of the day!"

"Remorse—why, Therese, remorse is just an illusion, merely the whining of a cowardly soul—too cowardly to stifle and kill it!"

"Can remorse be stifled?" asked Justine.

"Of course, nothing is easier, Therese. People repent only what they're not in the habit of doing. If you have remorse for anything you do, do it again and again, and you'll see how easily you forget about your conscience. And anyway who said that remorse proves a crime—it simply shows a weak soul, easily subdued. People have remorse for the most trivial sins. Crime is the most meaningless thing in the world, though sometimes necessary. All you have to do is convince yourself of this, Therese. Let us analyze what men generally call crime and you'll see for yourself. Isn't crime just violating the national laws and customs? But what is called a crime in France isn't one a couple of hundred miles from here. Is there any action considered criminal universally, by every nation on the globe? It is merely a matter of opinion, climate, location, taboos, Therese. What might be thought vicious and criminal here in France might be considered praiseworthy and virtuous elsewhere. And so isn't it absurd to try and force ourselves to practice virtues which are vice in some other place, and be afraid of committing crimes considered excellent actions in another country! Now, I ask you, Therese, why worry about having for your own interest committed a crime in France which is really a virtue in China? And why put yourself out doing good deeds they would hang you for in Siam? Can't you see that remorse doesn't spring from the act itself, but only because it is prohibited? Study the customs and morals of all nations, and you'll agree that remorse is the sole fruit of ignorance and prejudice. You'll learn that there is no real evil in anything and that it's stupid to repent and not do what is useful and agreeable to you. I am forty-five; I committed my first crime at fourteen and have never at any time been bothered with my conscience. When a thing didn't work out right I might have blamed myself for my awkwardness; but remorse—pff!"

"All right—I grant that, madame," Justine answered, "but let me reason according to your own logic. Why do you expect my conscience to be as firm as yours, since it has not been accustomed from infancy like yours to overcome the same prejudices? Why do you ask that my mind, so different from yours, be able to grasp the same theories? You yourself say that there is good and bad in nature—well there must be a certain number of people on the side of the good. That is the side I take, which is also according to nature. Then why do you want me to wander from the rules that that same nature which you worship so much lays down for me. Moreover, you mustn't think everybody is as lucky as you and always goes unpunished. You saw what happened to that gang of counterfeiters. Out of fifteen, fourteen died at the gallows in disgrace."

"Do you call that a disgrace, Therese? When one has outgrown these petty principles and childish prejudices he is indifferent to such meaningless things as honor, disgrace or reputation; and it makes little difference to him whether he dies on the scaffold or in bed. You see, there are two sorts of scoundrels in this world, Therese: one, who is rich and has power and influence; the law seldom reaches him. The other is *nobody* and, to make up for the immunity of the first scamp, the laws and authorities are doubly down on him. But, being born without wealth, if he has any sense he should have one aim: to get money anyway he can. If he succeeds he is a great success; if not, he is stretched on the rack. But what matter—he has nothing to regret as there was nothing to lose."

"I cannot bear to listen to your sophisms and blasphemies any longer!" Justine said, rising from the table indignantly.

"Just a minute, Therese!" said Madame Dubois, holding her back. "Sit down a minute, please—I want to talk to you—I want to help you! Listen, if you don't refuse to help me a little, here are a thousand francs—yours soon as the deed's done."

"What is it?"

"Did you notice that young merchant from Lyons who has been eating here the last four or five days?"

"Who, Dubreuil?" Justine asked.

"Yes, that's right!"

"Well?"

"He is in love with you," Madame Dubois said with a drop in her voice. "He has confided it to me. He thinks you're awfully nice. He thinks you are really beautiful, so modest and gentle and reserved. And I don't blame him, I think so myself. Well, this romantic young man is worth close to a million and his house is full of treasures. I want you to just let me make this man believe you like him too, and will listen to him. What do you say, Therese? I'll talk him into taking a walk with you and;; all you've got to do is amuse him and keep him out as long as possible while I rob him. I won't leave town immediately, and he'll never suspect us. Eventually, I'll leave quietly. You'll follow me and get your money once we're out of France. How about it, Therese?"

"All right," Justine fell in with her. Her real intention was to appraise Dubreuil of Madame Dubois' plans. And wishing to further mislead her she said, "But wait a minute! If Dubreuil is in love with me I can, on either warning him or yielding to him, get more from him than you're offering me to betray him."

"Good!" Madame Dubois answered. "You're learning— that's what I call a good pupil. I'm beginning to think you were more cut out for a career of crime than myself. Well, I'll make it five thousand then, is that better—are you satisfied now?"

For Justine the situation was very perplexing. Of course she had no intention of carrying out her agreement with Madame Dubois, for any amount of money. But to be compelled to expose Madame Dubois also grieved her. She hated to bring any creature into danger. What is more, she felt indebted to Madame Dubois for having ten years before freed her from prison. She very much preferred preventing the crime without anybody suffering for it; and with anybody but a consummate rogue like madame she might have succeeded.

It was all finally arranged, and that same evening Justine began putting Dubreuil more at his ease. She was convinced he really had a sincere liking for her. In short time a warm intimacy sprung up between them and they set a day to take a long stroll or ride together out into the open country.

On the day appointed Madame Dubois invited them both to have lunch with her in her room. After lunch, which was a long drawn out affair, they sat around a while and chatted pleasantly together. But Justine grew restless and said it was time for them to say goodbye and start out on their little jaunt.

They left Madame Dubois and went downstairs to get their horses ready; but before actually setting out Justine was alone a minute with Dubreuil.

"Dubreuil..." she said to him very quickly. "Listen to me closely.... say nothing.... do what I tell you! Have you got a reliable friend close by?"

"Yes, my partner—Valbois..."

"Good! Let us go at once and tell him not to leave your room a minute all the time we're out!"

"But I've got the key... why worry... why all this fuss...?"

"Do as I tell you, please—it's important—otherwise I don't go out with you. Dubois arranged this walk so as to rob you—she is watching us.... she's dangerous—hurry—give him your key and tell him not to leave until we're back—I'll explain everything later!"

Dubreuil did as he was cautioned, and after installing his friend Valbois in his room he set out with Justine. On the way out, at some distance from the inn, she gave him a lengthy explanation of everything and told him how she had become acquainted with a woman like Madame Dubois. And she also told him of all her unhappy experiences and misfortunes. He was very grateful land sympathetic. In a transport of emotion he offered to marry her. He told her that all her troubles were now over, and sketched for her in a faltering voice the fine life for many years to come that they would both have together. It was a flattering offer and she could not refuse it; but it seemed she could not accept it either without trying to make him see that all might give him cause to repent later his hasty offer. He was pleased with her delicacy and only pressed her the more eagerly.

The quick and embarrassed flow of their conversation had already carried them about three or four miles outside of the town. They were just going to alight and enjoy the cool shade of a wood along the river bank where they intended leisurely to stroll together, when Dubreuil suddenly said he was feeling very sick; and he leaned against the saddle and started to retch violently. They speedily drove back to town.

Dubreuil was so sick by the time they returned that he had to be carried to his room. A doctor then came and said he was poisoned. On hearing this Justine immediately ran to

Madame Dubois' apartment, but finding that she was gone, hastened directly to her own room and discovered it had been rifled, her money and clothes stolen. There was no doubt now in her mind who was behind it all.

She went back to Dubreuil's room, but was not allowed to come in. He was dying and very near his end. He was certain Justine was innocent and had expressly forbidden her being prosecuted.

Valbois, Dubreuil's friend, later came out and told her that it was all over. She wept bitterly and he tried to quiet her. He himself felt the loss of Dubreuil very deeply and sincerely. And though he pitied Justine when she told him of all her troubles and misfortunes, yet he blamed her for the over-tenderness which had hindered her from lodging a complaint as soon as she had been apprised of Madame Dubois' plans.

They both figured it would now be too late having Madame Dubois pursued, which would, moreover, involve considerable expense. And then again, her prosecution might embroil Justine. Valbois did not conceal from her the fact that if the whole of this last misadventure were made public the depositions he would be forced to make would compromise her, however guarded he might be, because of both her sudden intimacy with Dubreuil, and her last suspicious jaunt with him. He tried to impress upon her how easily she could be put under a cloud of suspicion. He thought it would be best to drop the entire matter and that Justine leave town immediately without seeing anybody at all. For his part he assured her that he would never act against her, and that in all that had occurred he believed her innocent and could only accuse her of feebleness. She then and there made up her mind and decided to do as he advised; it was certain even to herself that all appearances of guilt were against her.

"I'm sorry," Valbois said, handing her some money, "that

I can't help you much. I haven't an awful lot of money myself and can only spare a little. But I know a woman who is leaving here some time tonight or tomorrow for Chalon, which is my home town. I'll ask her to help you. Let me see—yes... right—come on, I'll take you to her right now, that's an idea, come on!" They both hurried out.

Introducing Justine to his friend and townswoman, Valbois said, "Madame Bertrand, this is Therese, a very good friend of mine. When are you leaving—tomorrow? Well, I want you to take Therese with you and look after her as if she were my own sister. She's going your way and is looking for work. See what you can do for her, will you? Don't charge her anything—I'll settle with you later. That's fine, thanks!"

He kissed Justine on the cheek. "Goodbye, Therese," he said, "Madame Bertrand is leaving early tomorrow morning. I hope you have better luck. I'll see you again soon. Goodbye!"

Chapter 21

JUSTINE FLOUNDERED in bewilderment before the sudden rush of events, and her heart was like a stone in her body. She wandered about the streets aimlessly, so shrunk with confused despair that she drew the attention of passersby; and to avoid the embarrassing and prying notice of others she made for the river bank, for some isolated spot where she could be alone with her thoughts and memories and free the clogging feeling in her breast.

There she sat for hours musing and thinking upon many sad reflections. As on many occasions before she also thought of her sister, Juliet; and wondered what had become of her, and if she, too, were so terribly unhappy. Justine had a terrible longing to see her, for she felt she now had to have someone to comfort her, but it made her miserable to think Juliet was gone forever out of her life.

So completely was she carried away by the current of her thoughts that the sun sunk beneath the water and the night's darkness soon spread over the town without her being aware of it. When three men got hold of her, one putting his hand on her mouth, only then was she roused from her deep reverie. They threw her headlong into a carriage which just then pulled up; and they sped through the town, going at the same pace for about twenty minutes.

The coach finally arrived at a house where they rolled through wide gates opened to let them in.

They crossed many long, dark rooms, in one of which, where a feeble light crept through the chinks of the door, they locked her in. A stout woman shortly came in with a candle in her hand. It was Madame Dubois. "Come," she said to Justine, "come, little innocence and receive the reward of your virtue." She pushed Justine impatiently into a room where an elderly man who had a face like a faun out of a Greek fable, but with a more stolid and not half so clever or lively an expression, was seated.

"Monseigneur," said Madame Dubois, pulling Justine in front of him, "here's the little girl you've wanted so badly— yes, the celebrated Therese, herself. There's nothing like her! She's a much better prize than the other little girl I'm bringing from the convent, who'll be here any minute, too. The other has physical virtues, but this one—ah! what sentiments! Sentiments are her whole existence, and you couldn't find a more frank or upright creature,—how about it, Therese! Both girls are yours and you can do whatever you want with them. But I've got to beat it—there's a man dead in this town and it's no longer safe here."

"No, no, darling!" said Monseigneur, "stay here. There's nothing to be afraid of—you're under my protection. How can I do without you.... but this Therese is really pretty...." And to Justine, "How old are you, my child?"

"Twenty-six, Monseigneur, and many sorrows."

"Sorrows... misfortunes—yes, I know all about it. Huh, it's amusing—really funnier than I thought it was. I'll put an end to all your troubles, my child—just twenty-four hours and it'll be all over. Isn't that right, Dubois?" he laughed.

"Of course!" Madame Dubois answered. "If Therese was not a good friend of mine I would never have brought her to you."

He made Justine lean her head upon his chest, and lifting her hair he closely examined the nape of her neck. He had hard bony hands with powerful fingers that gripped like a vise. "Oh, it's delightful!" he cried, vigorously pressing down on her collar-bone, "I have never seen one fastened so well—it'll be great fun slicing that head off!"

A knock was just then heard at the door, and Dubois went out and forthwith brought in the young girl from the convent about whom they had just spoken. Her name was Eulalie, a lovely girl to look at. "Good heavens, madame, where have you taken me!" she said. But Monseigneur was already pulling her roughly towards him, and with his long fingers proceeding to stroke her neck passionately. Wrinkling his forehead as if making some mental calculation, he sharply twisted her head from one side to the other.

"Come!" he said. "These two girls will give me great pleasure. You'll be well paid for this, Dubois. Let us go into my boudoir—come with us, Dubois, I want you to help me."

They were all compelled to go with him.

On a table to the right were many kinds of wines strong liquors and a great supply of food.

He took Eulalie first, and abetted by Dubois, his wild revel lasted for more than an hour. As Eulalie's severed head finally rolled heavily to the floor only then was he completely appeased. But he was completely exhausted, and staggered to the table and sat down.

It was his wish to prolong the agony of Justine's suspense.

He was in none too great a hurry; and he and Dubois drank heavily to revive their strength. But they sat at the table so long and gorged themselves with so much food and wine, making merry between them, that they eventually rolled to the floor blind-drunk. Justine, seeing this, grabbed whatever clothes were within reach, which happened to be Madame Dubois', and rushed madly out toward the stairs. Through the long empty apartments she stumbled and fell in the darkness; and on the other side of the corridor she heard a door slam and the dull tread of steps on the heavy carpets. She drew up rigid and clung close to the wall in the dark empty room, until the sound died away in the distance. She finally reached the gate without encountering any resistance, and got safely back to Grenoble.

It was very late when she reached town. But she immediately went to Valbois' room and knocked on his door. He woke up startled, and opening the door, his eyes swollen with sleep, he stared at Justine several seconds before recognizing her, such was the state she was in—what with the ghastly expression on her face and Madame Dubois' clothes all awry, hanging loosely about her. He asked what had happened, and gasping, she told him. "Can't you have her arrested?" she aspirated, "she's not far from here and I think I remember the way. The wretch! she took the money you gave me today, too!"

"God, Therese! you certainly are the most unfortunate girl in the world; something's always happening to you! No, we'll leave Dubois alone, for the same reasons I told you today. The less we mess with people of that sort, so much the better. The thing for you is to get out of this town. Here is some more money; there's enough for you to get some other clothes, too. Now, go and get some sleep and don't forget to meet Madame Bertrand early tomorrow. Good night, Therese, good luck."

"O virtuous young man...."

"Yes... good night, Therese, good night... good luck to you...."

Chapter 22

EARLY THE next day Justine left Grenoble. Though in that town she did not find the happiness she had always fancied she would, yet there at least she had received more pity than in any other, and that greatly consoled her.

Madame Bertrand and she were travelling in a small closed carriage driven by one horse. Madame Bertrand, a pretty nasty, suspicious, prattling, gossiping, troublesome, shallow-brained woman, was still suckling a little girl about fifteen months old. Everything went well right up to Lyons, where madame had to stop over for three days to carry out some of her business transactions.

In this town Justine had an encounter she was far from expecting. With one of the girls from the inn, whom she had begged to accompany her, she happened to be walking along the waterfront. A bright, clear day, they were enjoying the afternoon sunshine and watching the leisurely crowd of people go by. Suddenly, just a short distance ahead of her she espied the hermit Dom Antonin of the temple of Mota. Erect and beatific, he was walking gingerly towards her and she could not possibly avoid him. He bowed very grandly as he accosted her graciously in a low, smooth, unctuous voice.

"Therese, my child, how are you? Was that kind, running away like that? That wasn't nice, my child, leaving us the way you did! And who is this dear creature..." he addressed himself to the girl accompanying Justine, holding her chin paternally in his hand.

He told Justine that he was now first brother of the house of the Shaamanite Order situated in this town. He also said, in a low voice, that she ran great risk of being retaken by the temple in Burgundy if he merely sent word there. But he promised not to if she and her friend would come to see him in his new abode. He insisted that they come right along with him, that later they might have difficulty finding the place alone, as it was hard to get it. "We'll pay both of you well, Therese. We are ten in our house and I promise you at least a couple of francs from each one of us."

Justine blushed at these proposals and tried to make the idolater believe he was mistaken; but he was not to be put off. At length, upon her repeated refusals to follow him, he confined himself to merely asking for their address. To get rid of him Justine gave him a wrong number, which he jotted down in his pocket book. He left, assuring them that he would soon see them again.

Returning to the inn Justine explained to her companion, as well as she could, her acquaintance with the brother. But whether what she told did not satisfy the girl, who said, "I think he's awfully cute!" or, which is more likely, because the girl was vexed, having been deprived by Justine's virtuousness of an adventure bringing profit and pleasure—be that as it may, she tattled and told Madame Bertrand about it. Madame was greatly displeased, with Justine's virtue or lack of it is hard to say, and thereafter she seemed to nourish a ranking grudge against her.

They left Lyons very late and arrived at Villefranche about six in the evening. A long trip was ahead of them the next day and they were anxious to have supper immediately and go right to bed.

Many hours after retiring, the whole inn was aroused by great smoke which was rapidly filling all the rooms. The fire spread quickly, and Justine and Madame Bertrand, half naked, threw open their door. All about them they heard the deafening crash of falling walls, the cracking of timber breaking under the flames, and the shrill screams of people scurrying to safety. They were panic-stricken as the fire roared on all sides and they rushed haphazard through it and found themselves tied up with a knot of people, partly dressed and hysterical, trying to get out. Justine just then recalled that Madame Bertrand had forgotten her child behind in their room, and ran back and picked it up, holding it close in her arms. The flames were now raging more furiously; and she was burnt in several places, dodging falling plaster and timber, as she scampered back with the child in her arms to where Madame Bertrand was still huddled together with the same group of pushing men and women. Trying to step upon a half-burnt plank, her foot missed, and by a natural impulse Justine threw up her hands in front of her face, letting go of the child. It slipped from her grasp, and right under its mother's eyes fell and was buried under a heavy, falling, simmering debris. There was a terrifying scream as Justine felt herself dragged and pulled outside. In the general confusion she thought she was being dragged to safety; but when outside she found herself thrown into a coach where a woman dug a pistol into her ribs, she gathered her wits and recognized Madame Dubois staring menacingly at her. "You bitch! a word out of your mouth and I'll blow you out of your seat! I've got you now, and you won't get away again!"

"You here, madame?" Justine said, bewildered.

"You bet I'm here! That fire is my doings. It was through a fire I rescued you from jail and saved your life, and through a fire you're going to lose it! I would have chased you even to hell! I almost had you at Lyons—I just missed you! But I soon got on your trail again all right! I arrived here in Villefranche just an hour after you did. I knew you were in this inn and had my men set fire to it. I was going to get you dead or alive! You're going back to Monseigneur. He was furious when he learned of your getaway. He gives me a couple of thousand for every girl I get him. He was so mad he wouldn't pay me for Eulalie. We won't get out of this coach until we get to his house. And I'll teach you for robbing my clothes! And you just try and get away, you bitch!" Madame Dubois said furiously as the horses galloped rapidly on.

Chapter 23

THEY WERE CLOSE to getting into Dauphiny when six state troopers, chasing after Madame Dubois' coach, overtook them and, pistols in hand, ordered the driver to pull up.

Madame Dubois asked them with calm effrontery whether or not they knew whom they were handling, and what right they had using a woman of her station like that.

"We have not the honor of knowing you, madame," said the sergeant, "but we think you have a girl in your coach who yesterday set fire to the biggest inn at Villefranche. Here is her description, madame," he continued, staring hard at Justine. "I don't think I'm mistaken. Just hand her over tons and explain how a woman of your rank comes to be seen with such a dangerous person."

"There's really nothing remarkable about that," sail Madame Dubois, "I can easily explain it. You see, like hi I was stopping yesterday at that same inn at Villefranche, myself. I left in the midst of that confusion; and as I was getting into my coach this girl rushed up to me begging me to help her. She said that she had lost everything in the fire and asked me to give her a lift to Lyons. I felt sorry for her and hated to see the poor child stranded penniless. You see, gentlemen, my heart got the better of my reason, and I'm sorry for it now. Well, on the way she offered me her services. I thought I might be able to use her and was bringing her into Dauphiny, my family estate. It's a good lesson for me and I'll profit by it. Here, take her, gentlemen. I'm so glad the honor of my name will not be involved in such an unpleasant business, don't you know. Yes thank you, sir."

Justine attempted to defend herself and give Madame Dubois away; but her words were looked upon as slanderous recriminations, which Madame Dubois brushed aside with haughty contempt. "Quiet, you slut!" the sergeant bawled down at her; and she was immediately silenced. Was it possible that a woman like Madame Dubois, with such a display of wealth, coming from such a fine family owning large estates, could be guilty of a crime in which she appeared riot to have the slightest interest? And was not everything on the contrary against Justine? She was nobody; and she was penniless—it was quite certain she was in the wrong. What is more, the sergeant read Madame Bertrand's complaint; for it was she who accused Justine. The complaint read that Justine had set fire to the inn in order to rob Madame Bertrand more at her ease, which she had done to the last penny: that she had thrown the said Madame Bertrand's child into the fire so as to distract the said Madame Bertrand's attention from her maneuvers. The complaint also read that Justine was, moreover, a common prostitute, escaped from the gibbet at Grenoble, of whom the said Madame Bertrand had foolishly taken charge through complaisance for a young man from her own home town—one of Justine's lovers, no doubt: further, that Justine had publicly and in broad daylight accosted and enticed monks at Lyons, etc., etc.

They were ready to handcuff her. "But, sir," Justine said, before letting herself be taken, "if I had robbed Madame Bertrand the money must be on me. You can search me."

The sergeant laughed at this. He was sure, he said, that she must have had accomplices to whom she handed over the money before making away. "Anyway, you can tell it to the boss. Take her, men!"

The sergeant bowed deeply to Madame Dubois and said, "We apologize most humbly for having disturbed you in this way, madame."

While, without further ado, the other troopers dragged Justine out of the coach Madame Dubois slipped the sergeant several coins and he bowed again. He grew very gallant and obsequious as her carriage started to pull away.

The troopers soon arrived at Lyons with their prisoner. At the jail she was submitted to a thorough examination.

The evidence was that the fire had broken out in a hay loft, where several persons swore Justine had entered on the eve of the fire, which was true; Justine averred it herself. But she explained that, looking for a toilet, she had asked one of the servants of the inn, who had badly directed her to it. As a result, she had gone into the garret, and not finding the place she was seeking had remained there long enough to warrant suspicion. All which sounded vague and unsatisfactory. They were sure this was not her first crime; and found on examining her the mark branded on her shoulder by Rodin. Any further doubt was removed, and she was thrown into the criminals' dungeon, and her name entered into the jailer's book as an incendiary, a prostitute, an infanticide and a thief.

Alone in her cell, she wondered to whom in this town she could turn for help. Many names came into her mind, but most of them were total strangers, who more likely would be offended by her appeal to them, let alone bother themselves about helping her. There appeared to be no means of getting out of this mess; and the more she thought of her chances the more hopeless it seemed to her. But the name of Dom Antonin suddenly suggested itself to her mind and for a minute she had a ray of hope; but when she thought more closely of it her heart sank again with despair. But it bounded up again- for however slight the assistance she expected from him it was her only chance and she was going to gamble on if she couldn't resist it. Yes, maybe—maybe out of pity he would help her. She asked that he be sent for.

Dom Antonin came and pretended not to recognize her. But she told the keeper that it was indeed possible that he did not remember her, having guided her conscience only when she was very young; and that it was on this footing she sought a private conversation with him. The keeper was content and left them to themselves.

As soon as she was alone with the monk she rushed to his knees, and with a profusion of tears begged him to get her out of the scrape she was in. She tried to prove her innocence to him; and did not hide from him how the evil proposals he made her a few days before had turned against her Madame Bertrand, who was now her accuser.

He heard her very attentively, slowly shaking his head deprecatingly from side to side. "Therese," he said, "don't get so excited, as usual. It's a bad case, dear child. I might as well tell you, you're a lost girl—that's clear! All appearances are against you, and that's all that's necessary to convict you when you have no money and nobody knows you. But let me see... yes, there's just one thing can save you. I'm on intimate terms with the chief magistrate, and he can influence the judges of this town very much. I'll tell him you're my niece and will ask that you be sent away to your family. He'll have the case thrown out of court. Then I'll have you carried off. But you'll have to be shut up in our temple—you understand, Therese..."

"Go away!" she screamed. "You're a brute... to take advantage of my situation like that!"

"It's up to you, child," he said, taking his leave. "I never try to coax people to be happy."

As he was walking out Justine dragged herself back to his knees again and begged and pleaded with him to help her without such conditions. In the violence of her emotions her bodice was partly torn, and the swelling outline of her breasts was strongly accentuated, which, covered with tears and her disheveled hair floating over it, strongly excited the idolater. He pulled her to her feet; and threw himself headlong with her upon the shabby straw which served her as a bed. She tried to cry out, but he madly plunged a handkerchief into her mouth and completely overpowered her....

"Listen, child," he said, having risen and set himself to rights again, "you say you don't want my help; I'm sorry. If you say a word about what just happened here I'll tell them you tried to entice me, and they'll believe me, understand!"

And he called the jailer and said to him, "This foolish girl is mistaken. She meant a Dom Antonin who lives at Bordeaux. I don't know her at all—I've never set eyes on her before. But she begged me to hear her story and I have done so. Good day, sir."

Her last hope having faded, she grew bitter and sullen and indifferent to her fate; and nothing now mattered to her. But an hour after the outcome of her interview with Dom Antonin the thought that she was to be condemned as a felon by a judicial body rankled in her spirit. Anything but that—she preferred anything to this public disgrace; and this obsession of *public* disgrace made her think of Florent. And then she was quickly inspired with an idea; and already the upward surge of her hope dearly visualized to her the freedom before her. Yes, she would get in touch with Florent, a powerful man in this community, and she would accept the offer he once made her to enter his service, if he would but get her out of this complication with the authorities. Could she not pretend to enter his service at first, and later run away and get safely beyond his reach?

She procured some writing materials and wrote a short note cloaked in an air of mystery to Florent, asking him to come and see her; but did not sign her name.

When Florent arrived at the jail he was greeted with profound respect. He entered Justine's cell and drew up, "Oh, it's you!" he said with great offhand dignity. "I was mistaken by your letter—I thought it was somebody I couldn't imagine who; but an idiot like you. What is it you want now? You're guilty of a thousand crimes, and when I offered you an opportunity of earning your bread honestly you stubbornly refused!"

"I'm not guilty, sir!" Justine said quietly.

"You're not; if you aren't I wonder who is! The first time I meet you I find you among a gang of highwaymen who want to murder me; and now I find you in jail—I'd like to know what a man must do nowadays to be guilty!"

Justine tried to propitiate him. She said to him that now she would be glad to accept the offer he once made her; and be conscientious in her duties to him if he got her out.

He looked at her closely, pondered a minute, and said, "Well, I'll see what I can do. Your case will come up before Judge Cardoville; it rests completely in his hands. He is a very close friend of mine and I do lots of business with him. I'll speak to him about you."

And when he left without abusing her, Justine was extremely happy and hopeful.

The next day she was brought before Judge Cardoville for questioning. Judge Cardoville was a man over fifty with a gloomy and stern countenance. He was unusually big, and the great layers of fat on his person gave him the unmistakable likeness, as well as the pompous dignity, of an important diplomat, or a person of high official connection.

There were more than a hundred sworn affidavits against Justine; and when all the charges were clearly, established according to law, Judge Cardoville asked Justine whether she knew in Lyons a rich private citizen named Mr. Florent, one of the leading men of the city Justine replied that she did know him.

"Good!" Mr. Cardoville said, "that'll be all. This Mr. Florent, whom you admit to know, is well acquainted with you too; he has deposed that he has seen you among a gang of thieves wherein you were the first to rob him of his money and pocket-book. Your comrades wished to spare his life and you advised against it; but he managed to escape. This same Mr. Florent adds that, a few years afterwards, having recognized you in Lyons, he had allowed you to come and pay your respects to him at his house upon your promise of good conduct; and that there, while preaching to you, while trying to lead you into the straight and narrow path, you chose those sacred moments in which to rob him of his watch and a hundred francs lying on the mantel-piece!"

Justine was stunned by this overbearing flood of accusations, and maintained such a stupefied silence that the Judge ordered the clerk to write down that she admitted these charges by her silence and the expressions on her face. And so the case went at a great rate, and Justine was speedily condemned; and was to be conveyed to Paris to carry out the sentence.

Chapter 24

THE LATTER PART of the month Justine was to be taken to Paris. There were just a few more formalities to be gotten over with before the final execution of her sentence.

All through the trial and her period of imprisonment in the town jail she was the talk of all the local gossips in Lyons and the small villages lying close by. They deplored the bad times honest, right-minded folk had fallen upon. In the more fashionable drawing rooms women, not too rigid in their morals, surpassed one another in disparaging the clumsy machinery of justice that could so long delay bringing such an abandoned and dangerous criminal to bay; and they could not imagine how she could have been at large so long, gallivanting about through the country in the wake of crimes, robberies and fornications.

One day in the early forenoon a small hostile crowd gathered in front of the town jail to watch a notorious criminal being led amid jeers into a large coach heading for Paris. Justine was dressed in a short, shabby coat, and muffled up to the eyebrows with a large, dark taffeta mantle. She was bound, and was so weak she would certainly have fallen had not her guards held her up. And when the driver at last whipped his horses up and the coach started to crawl away, the crowd breathed more easily with a feeling of great security.

In the coach there were other passengers, besides Justine and her two guards, going to Paris, and other distant towns, that usual miscellaneous lot of men and women gathered from all walks of life as generally is to be seen in any public conveyance.

The roads were bad and the horses had great difficulty making much progress. And it was such a fine day, the sun so warm on the carriage windows, that many of the passengers were restless and impatient, huddled up in the close atmosphere of the coach with a notorious felon and started to grumble at the long delays.

Towards evening, a short distance from Montargis, the coach sprung an axle and had to pull off the road to the side. The driver and his man repaired it temporarily as best they could, and they just managed with difficulty to roll into the inn at Montargis. One of the men rode back on a horse to get another carriage and the passengers were forced to stop over for the night at the inn.

It is an amusement natural enough to watch people alighting from a coach; and as the carriage was emptying its passengers guests from the inn clustered in yard before its door, whispering together and speculating upon the kind of persons getting out: they expected usual an officer, a light o' love, and some monks. *So* everybody jolted out of the coach and it seemed then was no longer anybody left in it; but when a state trooper straggled out and received into his arms from one of his comrades inside a young woman bound as a criminal, deathly pale, the guests were taken aback, mournfully silent, and somebody in the crowd screamed, "Oh!... my god!....." A very pretty woman, richly dressed in the finest style, who appeared to be a lady of high rank, rushed up, shook Justine by the shoulders and looked closely into her face. "It's you, Justine... my dear sister.... you!" she wailed. "Don't you know me? Don't you know your own sister, Juliet!"

Justine did not at first recognize her sister; she had not seen her for years. But, nevertheless, Juliet placed her immediately, for there was an indefinable something in Justine's face that, once seen, could never again be forgotten— whether it was a peculiar wistful expression in her large pretty eyes, or the sad manner she had of holding her head, is hard to say; at any rate, she had a kind face, and one could never forget a kind face.

When Juliet rushed up to Justine, a dignified looking gentleman who appeared to be Juliet's husband followed closely at her heels. He was Mr. Hector de Corville, an important minister of state, very widely known. He disclosed his identity to the two guards and commanded them to unbind Justine, saying that on his own responsibility he would take charge of her. The guards, like almost everybody else, knew him very well, and in awe before his high authority, did as they were told.

Juliet and Mr. de Corville took Justine in to the inn and upstairs to their room. They brought her a little soup and something to eat. Then they told her to get some sleep and rest, that in the morning they would take her home with them to Paris, where Mr. de Corville would have her cleared of all guilt.

In the morning they set out in a private coach. On the way Justine told her sister with much sobbing all her sorrows and misfortunes.

Chapter 25

IN THE HANDS of her sister Justine was soon herself again, and her recent experiences were rapidly being blotted out of her mind.

Mr. Hector de Corville was making a thorough investigation of the fraudulent and unscrupulous methods and practices of judges and the smaller public officials. His exposures and efficiency stirred up quite a ferment of moral indignation. The body politic opened its eyes in wonderment that such conditions existed, albeit they had been going on since time immemorial, and set up a wild clamor for a general cleaning up of house. In the legislative halls Mr. de Corville made a speech that was the crowning achievement of his career, a speech that was one day to go down to posterity as a specimen of the world's most brilliant oratory. It was a speech that gathered momentum as it progressed, and reached the pinnacle of its eloquence in the peroration, in which he said: "Oh, my friends, the prosperity of crime is like the thunder, the deceiving fires of which embellish the atmosphere for an instant, only to hurl into the abyss of death, the unfortunate one they have dazzled!" It almost brought on a panic. It seemed inevitable that Mr. de Corville would be the next president of the new republic, such heights had he risen to these several weeks gone by.

But such was the moral atmosphere he was now wrapped up in that, like a contagion, it seemed to have spread to his mistress, Juliet, who told him that she was now contemplating leaving him, since they were living in sin and not bound together by the holy ties of wedlock. He pleaded with her not to, said it was never too late to make amends and that they would go to a priest right then and there. But she said she would give the matter a good deal of thought, as she was thinking of retiring into a convent. For ever since Justine was reunited to her, Juliet's remorse for her past life made her miserable; and when she read in the newspaper the printed contents of Mr. de Corville's speech she decided that every minute that it would be best for her to enter a convent and expiate the horrors of her past life.

Her life had been really very bad. When she left Justine some years before, she went forth into the world with no more resources than her younger sister. But in a comparatively short time she became, however, a titled woman, possessing an income running into hundreds of thousands, magnificent jewels, several mansions in town and country; and at the present moment she had the heart and fortune of Mr. de Corville, Minister of State, a man of tremendous power and influence, soon to be the first citizen of the country.

Her career, though, was a thorny one, surely nobody can doubt it: it is only through the most shameful and difficult apprenticeships that such young ladies can make their way.

Juliet's beginnings were particularly humble. On leaving Justine she had gone to a woman who was well known in the neighborhood and accosted her with her little bundle under her arm, a tattered blue gown on her back, hair disheveled, and the prettiest little figure in the world.

"How old are you?" asked Madame Hanscleaver, a woman of mixed extraction.

"Sixteen years old in a few days, ma'am," Juliet pertly replied.

"And never...."

"Oh, no, madame, I swear to you!"

"Sometimes in these days...—a seducer, a boy, a comrade, you know...—I want sure proofs," said madame.

"You can easily prove it yourself, madame..." Juliet answered, blushing.

Madame Hanscleaver clapped on a pair of spectacles, and having scrupulously scrutinized things fully to her satisfaction, she said to Juliet, "Come, little girl, you can stay here with me. Now if you're a good girl, and listen to my advice and do as I tell you, in ten years you'll be very rich and have your own business."

Madame Hanscleaver took Juliet's bundle and wanted to

know if the child had any money about her. The little lass shook her head, yes; and so madame asked her to turn it over to her, saying that she would save it for her, because it was bad for a young girl to have money, which only led to evil and temptation. "It is for your own good, my darling!" And she gave Juliet a long sermon; and then introduced her to her other companions in the same house. The room she was to occupy was pointed out to her. The very next day she took up her duties.

In four months her wares were sold to scores of persons. Some were content with merely the rose, but others, more finical, or eager, tried to blow out the bud blossoming aside. But every night Madame Hanscleaver straightened and set things in order, and during all the four months it was still the first flowers the knavish woman offered to the public.

At the end of this hard novitiate Juliet obtained the patents of lay-sister, and from that moment was really recognized as maid of the establishment and partook of its pains and profits.

But pride and ambition entered Juliet's soul, and she felt that she ought to go at large and cease languishing in a subordinate position. She longed for bigger fields to conquer.

An old and debauched lord who at first got her to come just for the business of a moment was soon very pleased with her, and she cleverly managed to get into his good graces. She soon appeared with an air of magnificence at the smartest fetes, along fashionable boulevards, and in all the haunts frequented by the highest society. She was admired, desired, and invited. In less than four years she ruined six men, the poorest of whom had an income close to a million. From then on her reputation was completely assured, her social position firmly secure.

Juliet had reached her twentieth year when a certain Count of Lorsange, a celebrated gentleman of fifty, fell so madly in love with her that he bestowed his name upon her and gave her an income of a hundred thousand, a mansion, servants, liverymen, a high esteem in the world which finally succeeded in having her debuts overlooked. But wishing to enjoy his name and fortune alone, she successfully did away with him.

She had become free and a countess, and as a rich widow she played a larger and larger part in the amusements of society. She gave fine supper parties, and into her house the most elite were only too happy to be admitted. Briefly she was a highly respected woman, notwithstanding she used to go to bed for two hundred, and by the month gave the gift of herself at five hundred up.

Up until twenty-four the Countess of Lorsange still made some brilliant conquests. She ruined three foreign ambassadors, two bankers, several brokers, a general, four cabinet ministers and had designs on the president.

Such was the state of affairs with Madame de Lorsange, when Mr. de Corville, a man of fifty who was way up in the world, was determined to sacrifice himself completely for this woman and attach her to himself forever. After considerable effort, by his constant attentions and untiring devotion, he managed to succeed, and he had been living with her close to four years when they ran across Justine.

And so it was not at all strange that Juliet was beginning to have such grave misgivings about the welfare of her soul, and that her nights were sleepless, spent in giving herself up to sickly, brooding humors. It is hard to conjecture whether or not her mind would have taken this turn did she not meet Justine, or had not Mr. de Corville worked upon her feelings by his impassioned speech; at any rate, she was indeed miserable, and was undecided between her affection for Mr. de Corville and seeking her salvation in a convent.

But several weeks later a tragic incident occurred that settled all doubt in her mind and finally determined the course of her future conduct. Mr. de Corville was then living in the country. One day an unexpected heat came oh and they were getting ready to go out for a long walk, Juliet, Justine and Mr. de Corville. All the windows and the doors leading to the porch were left wide open to let what little breeze there was come through. But thick, dark masses of clouds suddenly started to gather and a heavy storm was coming up. Lightning flashed through and the thunder boomed loudly and the wind shook the windows violently and almost tore the open doors off their hinges. Juliet was frightened and, her voice muffled by the deafening clamor of the wind howling around the house, she yelled to Justine, who was already close by the windows, to quickly pull them down. Struggling against the force of the wind, which almost drove her back, Justine tried to pull on one of the windows, when all at once a blinding bolt of lightning flashed through and laid her low in the middle of the drawing room. It had gone right through her breast and face. She was a pitiful sight to look at. Juliet screamed and fainted and Mr. de Corville called for help but it was all hopeless. Justine lay on the floor inert, the last spark burned out of her lifeless body.

Mr. de Corville ordered her to be taken out of the room, but Juliet, rising, firmly protested, "No, leave her under my eyes; I want to keep looking at her so as to strengthen myself in the resolutions I have taken." And for some time she was left alone gazing down at Justine who lay on the floor face up, black and ashen. She kept whimpering, "Oh Justine.... my poor darling, my poor Justine!"

Reader, this is a stark and tragic tale; but we hope that you have shed tears over the misfortunes of virtue and poor unhappy Justine will pardon the terrible sketches we were forced to draw so that you may, at least, reap from this story the same fruit as Madame de Lorsange. We hope that you will be convinced with her that true happiness lies only in the bosom of virtue. If God permits virtue to be persecuted on earth, it is not for us to question his intentions. It may be that his rewards are held over for another life, for is it not true as written in Holy Scripture that the Lord chasteneth only the righteous! And after all, is not virtue its own reward!

Printed in the United Kingdom
by Lightning Source UK Ltd.
130666UK00001B/13-15/A